"The very talented Muriel Jensen has a definite skill for penning heartwarming, humorous tales destined to remain favorites...."
—*Romantic Times Magazine*

Dear Reader,

Here we are in Dancer's Beach again with Peg and Charlie, parents of the McKeon brothers from the original WHO'S THE DADDY? series.

Also at the beach are the new residents of Cliffside, a home on the bluff outside of town. They are David Hartford, Trevyn McGinty and Bram Bishop—all recently retired from the CIA. They host a masked ball dressed as the Three Musketeers and cross paths with identical triplet sisters dressed as a Regency miss, a flapper and a southern belle.

Seven months later one of the women is rescued from the Columbia River very pregnant and suffering from amnesia. But which of the three sisters is she? And the question everyone is asking is *who's the daddy?*

I hope you enjoy finding the answer!

Best Wishes,

Muriel Jensen

*Don't miss FATHER FORMULA,
coming in January 2001!*

Dear Reader,

November is an exciting month here at Harlequin American Romance. You'll notice we have a brand-new look—but, of course, you can still count on Harlequin American Romance to bring you four terrific love stories sure to warm your heart.

Back by popular demand, Harlequin American Romance revisits the beloved town of Tyler, Wisconsin, in the RETURN TO TYLER series. Scandals, secrets and romances abound in this small town with fabulous stories written by some of your favorite authors. The always wonderful Jule McBride inaugurates this special four-book series with *Secret Baby Spencer.*

Bestselling author Muriel Jensen reprises her heartwarming WHO'S THE DADDY? series with *Father Fever.* Next, a former wallflower finally gets the attention of her high school crush when he returns to town and her friends give her a makeover and some special advice in *Catching His Eye,* the premiere of Jo Leigh's THE GIRLFRIENDS' GUIDE TO... continuing series. Finally, Harlequin American Romance's theme promotion, HAPPILY WEDDED AFTER, which focuses on marriages of convenience, continues with Pamela Bauer's *The Marriage Portrait.*

Enjoy them all—and don't forget to come back again next month when another installment in the RETURN TO TYLER series from Judy Christenberry is waiting for you.

Wishing you happy reading,

Melissa Jeglinski
Associate Senior Editor
Harlequin American Romance

MURIEL JENSEN
Father Fever

HARLEQUIN®

TORONTO • NEW YORK • LONDON
AMSTERDAM • PARIS • SYDNEY • HAMBURG
STOCKHOLM • ATHENS • TOKYO • MILAN • MADRID
PRAGUE • WARSAW • BUDAPEST • AUCKLAND

To Jeff and Cheryl at Coffee An'.
Thanks for all the fun over breakfast!

ISBN 0-373-16850-0

FATHER FEVER

Copyright © 2000 by Muriel Jensen.

Visit us at www.eHarlequin.com

Printed in U.S.A.

ABOUT THE AUTHOR

Muriel Jensen and her husband Ron live in Astoria, Oregon, in an old Four-Square Victorian at the mouth of the Columbia River. They share their home with a golden retriever/golden Labrador mix named Amber, and five cats who moved in with them without an invitation (Muriel insists that a plate of Friskies and a bowl of water are *not* an invitation!)

They also have three children and their families in their lives—a veritable crowd of the most interesting people and children. They also have irreplaceable friends, wonderful neighbors and "a life they know they don't deserve but love desperately anyway."

Books by Muriel Jensen

HARLEQUIN AMERICAN ROMANCE

*Mommy and Me
**Who's the Daddy?

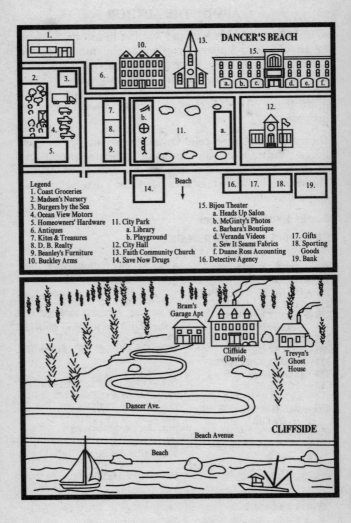

DANCER'S BEACH

1. Coast Groceries
2. Madsen's Nursery
3. Burgers by the Sea
10. Buckley Arms
13. Faith Community Church

Legend
1. Coast Groceries
2. Madsen's Nursery
3. Burgers by the Sea
4. Ocean View Motors
5. Homeowners' Hardware
6. Antiques
7. Kites & Treasures
8. D. B. Realty
9. Beanley's Furniture
10. Buckley Arms
11. City Park
  a. Library
  b. Playground
12. City Hall
13. Faith Community Church
14. Save Now Drugs
15. Bijou Theater
  a. Heads Up Salon
  b. McGinty's Photos
  c. Barbara's Boutique
  d. Veranda Videos
  e. Sew It Seams Fabrics
  f. Duane Ross Accounting
16. Detective Agency
17. Gifts
18. Sporting Goods
19. Bank

Beach

Bram's Garage Apt

Cliffside (David)

Trevyn's Ghost House

Dancer Ave.

Beach Avenue

CLIFFSIDE

Beach

Prologue

"I feel like someone in a crowd of suspects," Alexis Ames said to her sister Athena, "in the last scene of a murder mystery where the detective gathers everyone into a room and says, 'I've called you all here...'"

Athena smiled at Alexis's gravelly voiced imitation of a fictional detective. But as she looked around at the austere surroundings in the small law firm's conference room, she couldn't make the same connection.

They sat at a long, glass-topped table in a pearl-gray room whose color seemed to bring the gunmetal Oregon winter sky right indoors. Or maybe it was Aunt Sadie's death that made the world a dull, monochromatic place.

Athena shook her head. "Those things usually take place aboard a glamorous yacht, or in a warm library with a fireplace and antique furniture." Here there weren't even draperies on the windows, only chic vertical blinds in the same cold shade.

"And there are only three of us," Augusta, the third sister, argued in a hushed tone. "Hardly a crowd."

Alexis sighed. "I know, I know. And there hasn't even been a murder. Just a…death. Remember how Aunt Sadie always used to say she wanted to die in bed?"

Athena couldn't hold back a smile at the memory. "Yes," she replied. "And then she'd add, 'Mel Gibson's bed.'"

They laughed together for a moment, the first time they'd laughed since meeting at the airport hotel yesterday afternoon.

"I know it's small comfort," Alexis said, "but she died doing what she loved. Hawaii was her favorite place in the world. She loved relaxing in Lahaina and taking a plane to Oahu to go shopping for us."

"Yeah." Athena was unable to find comfort in anything. A woman in the prime of her maturity at just over sixty should not be entombed in the wreck of a tiny commuter plane at the bottom of the Pacific Ocean.

Sadie Richmond, long retired from a career as a Broadway dancer, had always provided the love, compassion and understanding that her sister—their mother—was incapable of giving. Athena and her sisters had spent spring breaks and summer vacations at her place on the beach where she encouraged them to explore their feelings, their talents and their hopes for the future.

"I can't believe we'll never see her again," Augusta whispered. She was the sensitive one who taught third grade and was in tune with her students. She wore an ankle-length flowered dress and strappy sandals. Her long red hair was piled into a loose bundle, tendrils spilling from her temples and the nape of her neck.

Alexis patted Augusta's knee. "I'll paint her portrait for you," she promised, then smiled ruefully, "if I ever recover my skills." Alexis was an artist and, if she was to be believed at the moment, an artist who could no longer paint. But she looked the part in a silky white blouse with billowing sleeves, and black pants and boots. Her hair, the dark-flame shade of red they all shared, fell to the middle of her back in ripples and waves. She wore no bangs and a frown now marred her forehead.

"It's just a slump and you'll get over it. No one can be brilliant all the time." Athena spoke with the same conviction she used in the courtroom. She was the practical one, the one who tried to have the answers.

Alexis gave her a look that said as clearly as words, *A lot you know. You don't have an artistic bone in your body.* Her eyes swept over Athena's blue suit and simple white blouse, over her hair caught in a thick knot at the back of her neck and added silently, *Just look at the way you dress.*

Athena didn't bother to argue. Her professional mode of dress helped her hold her own in negotiations and litigations dominated by men. It was an unfortunate truth that women who dressed with any style in the courtroom were often accused of doing so to distract or confuse.

She hadn't expected the severe suits to invade her private life as well, but now that she'd opened her own office, she had very little time for one anyway. And what private time she did have was spent in the company of other lawyers. However unconsciously, the sexless suit seemed to have become who she was.

As she studied her sisters, beautiful and curvaceous and alight with the gentle qualities of womanhood, she compared their attributes and appearance with her own steely determination to succeed. She felt as though they had acquired the womanliness she'd always admired in Sadie.

She'd wanted to be a lawyer even as a child, but she hadn't imagined that work would be the only thing in her life.

"Whoa!" Alexis whispered as a balding, mustachioed man pushed open the door. "Heads up! It's Poirot!"

The man's mustache was more of a simple brush than Poirot's elaborate handlebar affair, but he was dark and small and close enough in appearance to the fictional detective for them to appreciate the whimsy. Athena was grateful for the light moment considering their sad purpose in being here.

The man walked into the room with a sheaf of papers and stood across the table from the sisters as he introduced himself.

"Good afternoon," he said in slightly accented English that only served to heighten the Poirot effect. "Welcome to Portland. I'm..."

Then he seemed to forget who he was as his eyes

went from Alexis to Athena, back to Alexis, on to
Augusta, widening with every pass. "I'm, ah…"

"Bernard Pineau," Athena said, taking charge.
She'd been born nineteen minutes before Alexis, and
thirty-seven minutes before Augusta. She'd always
thought of herself as the eldest. "You're Bernard Pineau. Didn't Aunt Sadie tell you we're identical triplets?"

"She did, yes," he replied with a self-conscious
laugh. "But knowing that and seeing it for oneself
are two very different things. Please, pardon me for
staring."

Athena nodded. As children, she and her sisters had
grown accustomed to the gasps and stares their identical appearances created. But now with careers on
opposite coasts and Alexis on another continent, that
seldom happened. There were moments when she
missed it.

Athena introduced herself, then Lex and Gusty.

Pineau shook hands across the table and took his
chair.

"You must be the lawyer from Washington, D.C.,"
Pineau guessed, focusing on Athena. She wouldn't
have cared that he'd guessed, except that she knew
he'd done it after a glance at her suit jacket—all that
was visible above the table. It made her feel morose.

"Sadie was very proud of you," he added sincerely.

Resentment fell away and she experienced a moment's comfort. "Thank you."

He studied the other two women, then smiled at
Alexis. "You have the studio in Rome?"

Alexis nodded. "I do."

"I have your *Madonna 4* in my study at home," he said. "Sadie gave it to me for my birthday. My wife and I treasure it."

Alexis was surprised. "I'm glad. Aunt Sadie was my self-appointed PR person and one-man sales force."

"She was." He turned to Augusta.

"I'm the teacher," she said. "In Pansy Junction, California. Third grade. I love it."

He smiled indulgently at her. Augusta always inspired smiles.

Then he folded his hands atop the documents he'd brought with him and asked solicitously, "Would you like coffee before we begin?"

Three heads shook.

"We've just had lunch," Athena explained.

He nodded. "Then, before we begin, let me offer my condolences on the loss of your aunt. I met her just a year ago when we first worked on this will, and I found her to be a most charming and enlightened woman."

Athena opened her mouth to speak and discovered she had no voice.

"Thank you," Alexis said. "We did, too."

Pineau squared the pages on the table and began to read the formal legalese. "I, Sadie Richmond, being of sound mind..."

He read on and Athena and her sisters exchanged grim glances. There was no avarice here, no eagerness to know what Sadie had left to whom. Just a still profound disbelief that she was gone and a willingness to carry out her wishes.

"To Athena," the lawyer said, turning over a page, "I leave my Tiffany watch with the diamond fleur-de-lis in the hope that looking at it will brighten her tight schedule. I also leave her my aquamarine-and-diamond bar brooch to dress up her serious suits."

Athena closed her eyes and saw images of her aunt wearing the brooch on the shoulder of a smart black dress, on the lapel of her burgundy wool suit, on the blue blazer she'd worn to the Dancer's Beach Regatta every summer.

Tears welled in Athena's throat but she swallowed them.

"To Alexis," Pineau continued, "I leave my entire collection of berets because she always complimented me on them and has the flair to wear them, herself. And I want her to have the Degas in the upstairs hall because she might have posed for it."

Athena remembered the gilt-framed painting of a ballerina executing a grand jeté and thought the gift appropriate. Alexis always moved as though in ballet slippers.

A tear fell down Alexis's cheek and Augusta covered her hand with her own.

"To Augusta, I leave my doll collection and the Steiff bear she cuddled with when her sisters were too much for her."

Gusty nodded, her lips trembling dangerously. Alexis patted her back.

"I wish the girls to share whatever they would like of my clothes and my jewelry, then donate the rest to a women's shelter. I apologize to them for the paltry contents of my savings account, but they know how I've loved my travels. I wish it and my few stocks to be divided equally among them."

Pineau paused to take a breath.

Alexis and Augusta leaned back in thought and Athena let her mind drift to her favorite memory of Sadie. She was striding ahead of them up the beach at Cliffside, wearing pedal pushers and a T-shirt, her graying blond hair tied up in a scarf as she led them in the collection of shells and other ocean treasures.

Athena was lost in the moment, unaware that Pineau hadn't covered everything until he said, a little quickly, she thought, "And to David Hartford, I leave Cliffside and all its furnishings."

Athena's eyes flew open. She turned to her sisters and saw the same shocked surprise she felt mirrored in their faces. There was a moment of stunned silence, then a loud and simultaneous "Who?"

"David Hartford," Pineau repeated, tapping the document with the tips of his fingers. "A friend, apparently."

The women stared at one another again. Athena, caught completely off balance, struggled to think.

But Alexis didn't stop to think. "I've never heard of him," she said, leaning forward across the table. "A friend from where? Dancer's Beach?"

Pineau shook his head. "She didn't say where she met him."

"She never mentioned him to us." Augusta looked from one sister to the other. Heads shook confirmingly. "You have to contact him about the will,

Mr. Pineau,'' Athena pointed out, an unidentified but unsettling suspicion forming in the pit of her stomach where her grief for Sadie ached. "You must know where he lives. And why isn't he here?"

"I have contacted him. He lives in Chicago, but he wasn't able to come to the reading. So, I've faxed him everything he has to know, and transferred the house into his name."

Augusta and Alexis gasped simultaneously.

"When did Aunt Sadie change the will?" Athena asked. "We know that two years ago when we were all together at Christmas, she intended to leave Cliffside to the three of us. Not that we care about possession, but...it was a family home. Who *is* this guy?"

"This will..." Pineau began.

"What do we know about him?" Augusta interrupted. "I mean, she loved telling us stories about her life in Dancer's Beach. She lived very quietly, except for hosting some local events because Cliffside was so big. I can't believe she'd have become that close to someone without telling us. And if we've never heard of him..."

Pineau shook his head apologetically. "My job isn't to investigate the beneficiaries of a will, just to see that the deceased's wishes are carried out."

"When did she change it?" Alexis asked again.

"As I said before," Pineau replied patiently, "we drew up this will a year ago."

Athena stood in agitation. Alexis got to her feet and began to pace.

"I don't understand," Augusta said from her chair. "Where would she have met this Hartford guy?"

"Maybe on one of her trips," Alexis suggested, stopping in the middle of the carpet. "He's probably one of those gigolos who preys on older women and gets them to sign over their life savings. Or their house."

"Ladies, I know you're disappointed about Cliffside," Pineau said quietly, "but your aunt was very calm and clearheaded when she made the change. I think she truly wanted Mr. Hartford to have it. And I personally think she was too clever a woman to be fooled by a charlatan."

Athena frowned at him. "But we don't know for certain, do we, because you haven't conducted an investigation of any kind."

Alexis gasped and snapped her fingers. "Maybe he wants Cliffside for the smugglers' stairs!" she said to Athena. "I mean, apart from the fact that it's a wonderful property."

"That's right!" Augusta cried.

Pineau looked puzzled. "What stairs?"

"When we were children," Athena explained, "we discovered a door in the basement at Cliffside that led to a stairway through the cliff down to the beach. Sadie padlocked it, telling us that during Prohibition in Grandpa Richmond's day, booze had been smuggled in that way. Maybe Hartford is planning to put the house to a similar use. Drugs, maybe?"

"Ladies—" Pineau pleaded.

"I know, I know." Athena cut him off. "It's not your job to check him out, but maybe it's ours. Think about what's happened here! Our aunt dies in the crash of a light plane shortly after she wills the family home to a total stranger?''

''It's been a year since she changed the will,'' Pineau pointed out again, reasonably. ''We have no reason to believe the plane crash wasn't a simple accident. And Hartford wasn't a stranger to her.''

She ignored his attempt at reason and turned to her sisters. ''Until the authorities can bring up the plane and prove to me that the crash was an accident, I think this Hartford bears looking into. What do you say?''

Augusta nodded. ''Let's do it. I took a couple of weeks' leave.''

Athena turned to Alexis. ''What about you, Lex?''

Alexis shouldered a large soft leather pouch. ''My time's my own. I'm in. Where do we start?''

''What's Hartford's address?'' Athena asked Pineau

Pineau tapped the document on the table. ''As of the moment I notified him, his address is Cliffside, Dancer's Beach, Oregon.

Chapter One

David Hartford surveyed the wide living room of his new home and thought it looked comfortable, if not exactly true to a period or a style. He'd put some of the pieces he'd inherited into storage to make room for some of his own things. When he had time to think about it, he'd decide what to do with them.

It had been a week and a half since Aunty's attorney had called him to let him know he'd inherited a two-acre estate overlooking the Pacific Ocean and he still couldn't quite believe it. He'd grown up in a house three times this size, but it had never been a home, and he'd never felt as comfortable in it as he did here after barely a week.

His inheritance included this twelve-room Colonial Revival home, a guest house, an apartment over a four-car garage, and a small forest of firs, ash and oak tucked around the back of the property in a half-moon embrace. A shaggy lawn stretched thirty yards in front of the property to the edge of the cliff that rose fifteen feet above the ocean. Shrubbery he couldn't identify provided protection from the cliff's edge.

And it was all thanks to the gratitude of a woman

he'd never met, a CIA agent code-named Aunty who'd been his phone and radio contact on several jobs for the Company. He'd helped save her life in Africa when she'd been trapped in the path of a rebel advance, but he'd called in mercenaries to bring her out, so technically, *they'd* saved her life. That detail hadn't mattered to her, according to Aunty's attorney, who'd notified him of his windfall.

David was grateful, of course, and aware that the gift couldn't have come at a more fortuitous time.

Life as a CIA agent had lost its glamour for him and his team after the fiasco in Afghanistan, and now the three of them were starting over as "civilians."

So the large, comfortable furniture from his Chicago apartment now sat among a little round mahogany table, an old Windsor piano from the turn of the century, a curio shelf that now held his collection of hand-carved decoys. A large armoire removed from the bedroom had become a perfect entertainment center. The attorney had sent him a list of things willed to other beneficiaries and David had those shipped off to him.

He punctuated that observation with a sneeze. He held a folded handkerchief to his nose and thought it ironic that someone who'd survived spring and summer in Illinois as a boy without succumbing to allergies should be felled by the mold and mildew of an Oregon winter. Trevyn McGinty and Bram Bishop walked through the open front door, each with an armload of folding chairs borrowed from city hall's meeting room.

"Are you going to help us?" Trevyn asked, moving on through to the dining room and shouting back over his shoulder, "or are you just going to stand there and congratulate yourself on making points with the mayor of Dancer's Beach just two days after moving to town?"

Bram followed Trevyn with a tauntingly disparaging glance in David's direction. "He's going to stand there," he said. "He thinks that just because he's letting us live with him for a couple of months that indentures us somehow. Tell us again—" his voice rose as he went into the other room "—how we ended up having to host a party for two hundred people when we know absolutely no one here!"

There was the clatter of metal on metal as they began to open the chairs.

David pocketed his handkerchief and went into the large dining room that accommodated a table that seated twenty. For the purpose of the party, he'd distributed those chairs around the living room and placed the table at the side of the room for buffet service.

He helped place folding chairs. "Because Aunty always hosted the historical society's masked ball every year and her...passing left them high and dry a mere ten days before the party."

They exchanged grim glances. Trevyn and Bram had worked with Aunty, also.

Trevyn sighed and looked around the room. "She was so no-nonsense on the job," he said with a reminiscent smile. "It's weird to think that she had this beautiful home and willingly left it for...what? We were looking for excitement, but what is a sixty-year-old woman looking for?''

''Some kind of fulfillment, maybe,'' Bram guessed. ''You could tell by the way she worked she wasn't the kind of woman who did nothing but golf.''

They were all quiet another moment, then he put a chair in place and asked briskly, ''There's no Elk's hall or armory or anything in town where they could have had this affair? They had to have it here because that's the way they've always done it?''

David shook his head. ''Invitations had already gone out. Many to out-of-town people who are summer residents of Dancer's Beach. Calling to change locations would have been too complicated. So the mayor stopped by while the two of you were still driving the U-haul in from Chicago and asked me if I'd consider saving their hides. Since all three of us will be doing business in this town in one way or another, it seemed like the sporting thing to do.''

Trevyn unfolded the last chair. ''What do you know about these historical society types?''

David stood back to survey their work. ''Not much, except that I imagine they'll be Mrs. Beasley's vintage—middle sixties—so don't get your hopes up for a lap full of beautiful young things. But they might prove to be potential clients for your photo studio.''

''Hope so.'' Trevyn flattened the seat of a chair in a corner, his expression suddenly serious. ''I can't believe Aunty left you all this—or how lucky *we* are that you're still looking out for us even though we're not in the field anymore.''

David moved a floor lamp aside several inches to

make room for the chair. "We've been on so many rotten jobs together, it seems like now that we get to live real lives, we ought to at least start out together."

They'd shared experiences over the past few years that made men closer than brothers. In good times, they'd been an efficient, effective machine that did the government's dirty work.

In bad times, they'd shared one another's pain, nursed one another's wounds, and on a few occasions, saved one another's lives.

The experiences made transitioning into normal, everyday life difficult. And an exercise best shared with friends. "Well, how come he got the guest house and I got the room above the garage and a daily dose of carbon monoxide?"

Bram was putting him on. He'd done his job fearlessly on their last mission when everything had gone bad on them. He was a couple of years older than Trevyn and David and had seen far more action—too much, maybe—but there wasn't a selfish bone in his body.

"It keeps you out of the way," David replied. "You know, like the crazy relative nobody wants to talk about."

"Would you really rather have the guest house?" Trevyn asked Bram, still serious.

Bram shook his head at Trevyn, then grinned at David. "He's so easy. No, I don't want the guest house. I'm very comfortable in my apartment. I don't need a dark room and space to store all the contraptions you've got. I've got my office downtown and when I come home, all I need is room for the television, a coffeepot and a bed.''

The three loped out of the house to the truck Bram had used to pick up the chairs from the party supplier. There were another dozen to unload. A pewter sky spit rain and blew a cold wind around them.

"Did I tell you I got a case?" Bram asked as he leaped into the truck to hand chairs down. "It's just a divorce case surveillance, but detective work has to start somewhere."

"At least you found an office and got it open in three days." Trevyn took two chairs in each arm and started backing toward the house. "I've found a photography studio, but it'll be weeks before I get it in good enough shape to open the doors." He turned and hurried into the house with his burden.

David watched him go, concerned about his carefree attitude, so at odds with the burden he carried inside.

"He's going to be all right. Stop worrying," Bram said, handing David down a pair of chairs.

"He won't talk about the mission," David disputed. "That isn't healthy."

Bram grinned at him. "You're a writer," he said. "You have to understand everything. You have to know every little detail and how it relates to every other one. But some of us aren't like that. We just let it be and go with it. He's healing. His nightmares have stopped. He no longer gets times and places confused. Stop worrying."

David walked back to the house with the chairs, thinking Bram was right. The three of them had been living in David's Chicago apartment since their "retirement" two months ago and he and Bram had been awakened half a dozen times by Trevyn's nightmares of that last mission.

David and Trevyn had been paired up by the CIA years ago, the natural combination of a writer and a photographer to seek out intelligence and bring back information. They'd held regular jobs between CIA assignments, David writing a column for the *Chicago Tribune,* and Trevyn working as a photojournalist. The publisher, an old military man, knew about their part-time work for the government.

On their last mission, they'd been sent into Afghanistan to track Raisu, an infamous terrorist thought to be hiding somewhere in the Paghman Mountains north of Kabul.

Bram, a security expert with fifteen years in the military and five with the Company, had been assigned to keep them safe.

They'd hired a young native man as their guide, and his sister as their translator. Bram hadn't liked their dependence on anyone outside their small unit, but the terrain and the language were difficult and they'd had no choice.

Trevyn had formed a particular attachment to Farah, the translator, and when she'd wanted to go ahead of them to provide a distraction as David and the team approached, Trevyn had refused her. But despite all they'd heard about male dominance in Middle Eastern cultures, it apparently hadn't applied in her case. She'd gone ahead of them anyway.

The whole thing had gone to hell within a minute of their arrival. She'd been one of the first to die.

Their escape had been a grisly ordeal. When they'd finally reached Pakistan and safety, Trevyn didn't speak for days afterward.

They'd been debriefed, then all three had resigned.

Bram had no life to go back to, and Trevyn, though now pretending to be his old self, had seemed fragile to the two of them. By mutual consent, the three decided to stay together until they could decide what to do with the rest of their lives.

The *Chicago Tribune* had called David wanting to know if his award-winning social observations column would begin the following week.

As he thought about it now, it was odd how clearly he'd known he could never go back to that column. With wit that had been a gift from his father, and charm that was half natural, half manufactured, he'd written columns three times a week on life in Chicago.

He'd done it kindly, warmly, affectionately, as though life in Middle America was the most important thing in the world.

But since Afghanistan, he was less intrigued and amused by life than he was weary of what people did to each other. He had a perspective—more suited to the novel he'd been working on in his spare moments for the past year and a half. It was based on personal experience but fictionalized to protect the security and anonymity of the Company.

He found that he had a new confidence, and a new vulnerability that made him at the same time brave and uncertain—a good perspective from which to create a fictional hero.

In the house, Trevyn took the chairs from him and pointed to the large country kitchen that opened off the dining room. "Should we put chairs in there?" he asked. "Just to make sure we have enough seating?"

"Sure." David pointed to the far end of the kitchen, where a sofa and a lamp made a small reading area. "Put them there, so they won't be in the caterer's way."

Trevyn did so, and when Bram returned with the last of the chairs, he set them up opposite the sofa.

"So, you were telling us," Bram said with a grimace, "there will be *no* single women at this do?"

David shrugged. "Maybe. The whole town is invited, so if there are beautiful, unattached women around who have nothing better to do on a rainy Saturday night than attend a party thrown by the historical society, your dream woman might just appear."

"What's she like?" Trevyn asked. "Black belt? Rapid-fire pistol champion?"

Bram grinned. "While strength is sexy, I want a woman who makes love not war. I've had it with conflict."

"Amen," Trevyn agreed. "I want one who finds me irresistible."

"And on what planet would that be?" David asked.

Trevyn gave him a mirthless smile. "I'd take exception to that, but you're my landlord. What else do we need to do?"

David shook his head. "Nothing. Go relax for a while. Does the costume fit?"

"Pretty well. The sleeves are a little short, but the ruffles cover it." He frowned good-naturedly. "I can't believe I'm doing this for you."

"You're doing it for yourself. Remember the historical society people are a good connection for you. Think of all those grandchildren they'll want you to photograph. Your costume fit, Bram?"

"Yeah," Bram replied. "Thanks to the fact there are no orangutans in *my* family, my sleeves fit fine."

"Funny." Trevyn headed for the door. "When are the caterers arriving?"

"About an hour before," David replied. "Six or so."

Bram followed Trevyn out the door. "Hoping to find your dream girl and a great cook all rolled up into one?" he asked.

Trevyn's answer was bitten off by the closing door.

David went upstairs to shower, but he hesitated by the master bedroom window to look out on the ocean that stretched to the horizon.

He used to have a dream girl, he thought, as he watched the quiet sheet of gray silk, nothing moving on its surface but one lone seagull bobbing with the waves.

A woman he'd thought filled those requirements had been part of his life until last summer when she'd left him. She'd been a dramatic brunette, intelligent and sophisticated, and as work driven about her post as women's news editor as he was with his column.

They'd had an ugly fight when his young brothers

had come to visit and she'd considered it an imposition on her social schedule. He'd realized then how little he'd meant to her, except as an escort people noticed.

Now he had a completely different vision of the woman he wanted to share his life. Someone warm and soft who could laugh and smile and to whom sophistication didn't mean being scornful of everyone who didn't have it.

But would that kind of woman want him?

He'd changed a lot over the past few years. He had dark places in his soul. He had memories that were hard to live with. He had hatreds.

He tore himself away from the window and headed for the shower, telling himself that Dancer's Beach was his opportunity to change all that. And he had friends to help him—friends who had things they wanted to change, too.

And maybe he'd get lucky about the woman.

It could happen.

Chapter Two

"I want to go on record as saying this is insane," Gusty said from the back seat of a little blue import Athena had rented when they'd first arrived in Portland. "And that I want to know the truth about these guys as much as you do, but I'm just not sure I can carry off the plan."

Athena sighed into the rearview mirror, in no mood for Gusty's naive sense of morality. Most people thought it came from dealing with young children, but Athena had known Gusty had this flawless moral compass since she'd been a child herself. Right now, though, she looked more like a conscience-stricken Scarlett O'Hara, sitting moodily in a corner of the back seat, the hoop skirt of her green dress poufed out around her. She fiddled with the ribbons of the green bonnet in her lap.

Her costume was part of the plan.

"Gus," Athena made herself say patiently. "We have to go to this party, otherwise we'll never know if Aunt Sadie's death was truly an accident. If she gave the house willingly to this Hartford guy, or if she was coerced. You can do this."

"It's dishonest."

"So are they."

Athena had received a fax yesterday from Patrick Connelly, a detective who did work for her office and whom she'd asked to check out David Hartford. After waiting a week with her sisters in a downtown hotel, she'd found Patrick's fax contained confusing and unsettling news.

David Hartford, thirty-four, graduate of exclusive Claremont School for Boys, of U.C.L.A. with B.A. in Sociology, *Chicago Tribune* columnist since 1991. Took up residence at Cliffside a week ago, according to public utilities services established in his name. Two friends or associates also in residence.

Trevyn McGinty, 32, B.A. in Journalism from Cornell. Camera bum until hired by *Chicago Tribune* in '93.

John Bramston Bishop, 37, born in Boston, joined U.S. army at eighteen, served ten years until age twenty-eight. No information until current address.

Athena—strange gaps in more recent information on all three. Part of the reason this took so long. Curious, unexplained absences. For long periods, it's almost as though they cease to exist. Best I could do on short notice.

One more interesting detail. Hartford is hosting the local historical society's annual masked ball fund-raiser, usually held at Cliffside. According to an article in the paper eulogizing your aunt and "canonizing" Hartford, Mayor Beasley of Dancer's Beach asked him to host the party since your aunt's death left the event homeless. He generously agreed. He's either a pillar-of-the-community type anxious to fit right in, or a supremely deft con artist.

Notify if you want me to pursue.

Pat.

"Oh-oh," Lex had muttered as she read over Athena's shoulder. "Now there are three of them at Cliffside?"

"What kind of *absences,* do you suppose?" Gusty asked over Athena's other shoulder. "I wonder if they went to prison, or something."

Athena shook her head. "That would be on record. It's the criminals who don't get caught who know how to cover their tracks. Damn it." She'd hoped the information would be more definitive so she could contact the police and charge the new owner of Cliffside with something substantial.

Obviously, she was going to need more information before she could do that, and it was going to take a hands-on approach.

"We're going to the costume party," Athena had said authoritatively.

"Oh, no," Augusta had groaned.

But Alexis was in agreement and, as had happened throughout their childhood, Augusta had been forced to go along or be left behind.

They'd reached the coast by noon the following day, and found a costume shop in Lincoln City not

far from Dancer's Beach. The chatty clerk told them
the historical society party was responsible for the
thin selection of costumes left. Then she added, without realizing how they valued the information, "The
hosts will be dressed as the Three Musketeers."

"We're not going to get away with this," Augusta
complained anew. "Some of these people might remember us as children."

"The masks will conceal our identities," Athena
argued confidently. "We came here a few times as
adults, but usually on such quick visits, we never even
got to town. If anyone saw us all together, or if we
were dressed the same, they might recognize us, but
we'll be dressed differently and our eyes will be covered."

Alexis frowned. "What difference does it make if
we're recognized or not?"

Athena glanced impatiently at her sister. "If we're
recognized, then Hartford and his friends will know
who we are and whatever information they might
have shared with us is down the tubes."

Alexis made a face. "And you think if they *don't*
know who we are, they'll eagerly tell us they've coerced an old woman into leaving Hartford her
house?"

"No," Athena replied with a huff, "but if they're
being hit on by women who flatter them and hang on
their every word, they might loosen up and let information slip."

Gusty groaned, "I hate this."

"Got to give you credit," Alexis said, patting

Athena's shoulder. "That's a plot worthy of Mom's manipulative schemes."

Athena bristled but remained calm. She had a lot to do tonight, and she couldn't do it with half her mind distracted by old sibling rivalries.

Then Alexis continued. "You remind me a little of her lately with that severe expression when you're..."

That did it. Athena pulled over, the surprised driver behind her leaning on his horn as he swerved around her on the wet road.

Athena glowered at Alexis. "I bear no resemblance whatsoever to Mom," she said loudly. "But if you think so, you can just get out of the car!"

Alexis blinked at the outburst. "Calm down. It was a harmless obser—"

"You're never harmless!" Athena shouted. "You're always likening me to Mom in subtle little ways and you know I hate it!"

Alexis's mouth settled into a grim line. She unlocked her door. "Fine," she said stiffly. "I'll just..."

As she tried to open the door, Gusty reached over the seat and locked the door. "Come on, Athena," she said quietly. "Lex didn't mean it." She gave their sister a scolding look. "You know how she is."

"*I* don't," Alexis retorted. "How am I?"

"Determined to blame us," Gusty said quietly, "because Mom wasn't the mother you wanted her to be. You were always sure that if it had been just you alone, she'd have loved you. You think we crowded that out, but we didn't. She just didn't have love in her."

Alexis folded her arms and stared out the windshield. "That's a little oversimplified."

Augusta shrugged. "Most things that are big on the outside come down to one very simple thing on the inside."

Athena, a little startled by that profound observation, leaned back with a sigh as traffic sped past.

"You pick on Athena most," Augusta went on, "because Mom loved her most—or, at least as much as she was able to love anyone. She thought you were a dreamer and I was a coward. She had no use for us."

Athena closed her eyes, trying to blot out the memory of that beautiful woman who'd failed them at every turn.

"What does it say about us," she asked no one in particular, "that she still dictates our behavior toward one another after all these years?"

"That we're normal," Augusta replied. "A lot of people don't have anyone to work through the past with."

Alexis frowned at her. "I hate it when I'm angry and you just flatten out the source of it with logic and understanding."

Augusta smiled in the face of her exasperation. "No, you don't. You really love me and Athena, you just deal with your own rejection by trying to reject us in return. But we're here for you whether you like it or not."

Alexis turned to Athena, a new alliance formed in their amazement over Augusta. "Where did this

Pollyanna come from?'' She shook her head. ''I can't in all conscience leave you alone with her.''

Athena felt the turmoil always created inside her by the mention of their mother settle down into the acceptance she always thought she'd mastered but hadn't quite.

''Okay. But, I'm not like her.'' She didn't have to specify who she meant.

''I know,'' Alexis replied. ''I'm just...jealous.''

Athena raised an eyebrow in astonishment. ''Of what?''

''Your ability to get on with it. I still wonder all the time what I did wrong.''

''The same thing we all did,'' Athena replied. ''We challenged her position as most beautiful and adored. We didn't mean to, but we were born with her looks and we were children. We stole the show. She couldn't forgive us for that.''

''And she couldn't love us,'' Augusta finished. ''It's nothing we did. The sooner we all come to terms with that, the sooner we find relationships, let love into our lives. Move on.''

''After we get the truth out of the Cliffside gentlemen,'' Athena said. She reached a hand toward each of her sisters. ''Agreed?''

''Agreed.''

''Agreed.''

They stacked hands in the ritual sharing of an oath—in the tradition of the Three Musketeers.

ATHENA STOOD on Cliffside's wide doorstep, tugging at the neckline of her Regency period gown. Her hair was partially concealed by a beaded cap that left only a few red tendrils showing.

The cut of her gown made her bosom swell above the low neckline and she was wishing that the costume had come with a shawl.

Lex pulled her hand away.

Athena held up her white silk mask while Lex tugged down on the neckline of her dress. "I thought you wanted him to be so captivated by you that he'll tell you everything. Showing bosom does that to a man."

"Easy for you to say." Athena indicated the relatively high neckline of her simple, slip-style flapper dress. "You're covered."

Lex put her fingertip to the hem of the dress that fell above midthigh. "If I showed any more leg, this would be a chemise!"

Gusty fidgeted with the strings of her bag and looked anxiously toward the window where revelers could be seen laughing and dancing.

"Relax!" Athena ordered. "You're going to be fine. You look so sweet and innocent, the one you get will spill his guts to you."

The door was opened by a pretty but considerably mature Marie Antoinette who'd eaten a little cake herself.

She looked first surprised, then smiled widely. "You must be those pretty girls in the chamber of commerce office!"

Athena, Lex and Gusty smiled in unison.

Marie Antoinette opened the door wider, inviting them inside.

Athena felt a virulent stab of nostalgia. The house was so familiar and...not. She looked around her and recognized the armoire that had been upstairs, the little round mahogany parlor table. But the sofa and chairs were new, as was the artwork on the walls.

And the duck decoys.

Nostalgia turned to anger—and that steadied her and brought her back to her purpose. What kind of a mean man would hunt ducks?

The same kind who'd cheat a helpless old woman out of her house!

"Food's in the dining room." Marie Antoinette pointed with a fan that appeared to be Japanese. Then she tapped it against her chin as she surveyed the room. "Let's see if I can find you one of our hosts."

"Oh, don't worry about us," Athena said. "You go back to the party."

"I can't just leave you..." she began to protest, then the doorbell rang.

Lex shooed her toward the door. "Go. We'll be fine."

"I'm not fine," Gusty said under her breath when Marie Antoinette went to the door. "I'm terrified!"

"Just stick to the plan," Athena said patiently. "Make friends with him, try to draw him out. If it doesn't work, simply wander away. We'll all meet back at the car at the bottom of the driveway."

Lex closed a cold hand over Athena's arm. She pointed discreetly toward the far edge of the living room where a Musketeer was surrounded by a pair of cowgirls, Abraham Lincoln, and *Star Trek: The Next Generation*'s Captain Picard.

''There's one,'' she whispered.

''Go, Gusty,'' Athena said. ''Before you lose your nerve.''

Gusty closed her eyes, drew a deep breath, gathered up her skirts and floated off in his direction.

Lex turned to Athena in surprise. ''She did it! I didn't think she'd do it!''

''Of course she did it. She always comes through for us. She's just not as foolish as we are. Look!''

Athena turned her sister toward the kitchen from which a Musketeer emerged with a champagne glass in each hand. Without prompting, Lex placed herself in his path. ''Hello!'' she said. ''Is one of those for me?''

The Musketeer handed her the glass and gave her his full attention as she tucked her hand in his arm and began to chatter as they walked toward the sofa.

Athena wandered through the dining room, then the kitchen, in search of the third Musketeer. Her heart was pounding in her chest. Though she'd denied it to Gusty, this scheme was chancey, but since the direct approach wouldn't work, she couldn't think of any other way to find out who David Hartford was, why Sadie had left him her home, and whether or not he'd had anything to do with her death.

DAVID TOOK ANOTHER antihistamine, knowing it would do nothing to combat the exhaustion he felt. After being up half the night getting ready for the party, a pill that would make him even drowsier was the last thing he needed. But he'd been sneezing nonstop since before the party started half an hour ago, and he was afraid he was besmirching the heroic image of the literary Musketeer.

He replaced his itchy wig, adjusted his beard and mustache and put on the mask. Then, with a flourish to put himself back in character, donned his hat.

He was halfway down the stairs when he spotted her.

From his vantage point some distance above her, all he could see was red hair trapped in some kind of beaded net, the tip of a pert little nose, and the soft, beautiful swell of breasts rising out of the top of her dress. The breath caught in his throat and his heart lurched. For a moment he couldn't move. All he could do was stare down on her and take in the exquisite perfection of the view.

Then she turned as though she sensed his presence and caught his eye.

Not that he could see hers, or she his—not behind the masks. But there was something in the way she turned to look up at him, something in the small smile that curved her lips that told him she'd been waiting for him.

Probably not deliberately, but now that she'd seen him, she wanted to know him. Just as he wanted to know her.

He walked down the stairs and around the railing to where she stood. He removed his hat, again with a flourish, and gave her the bow he'd seen in movies.

"Mademoiselle," he said. "D'Artagnan at your service."

She smiled teasingly. "Technically, D'Artagnan wasn't one of the 'three' Musketeers."

He made a tsking sound. "But we're not being technical tonight, we're being fanciful."

"My apologies, monsieur." She curtsied, arms gracefully held out. "I am...Constance."

Well. D'Artagnan's love. She was willing to play his game.

And the rest of her—what he could see of her— was just as beautiful as his aerial view had been.

Her face was oval shaped, her lips like a small heart above a pointed little chin. She wore a black ribbon with a cameo on a slender neck fringed with fiery red tendrils of hair that had escaped the beaded head-piece.

He peered into her mask. "Blue or green eyes?" he asked. "Ah. Blue. Dark blue. But no freckles with that hair?"

She laughed lightly. He loved the sound of it.

"No, mercifully," she replied. "Though there are a few on my back."

"You must show me," he teased.

At which point she turned and obligingly lowered her head, revealing slender shoulders dusted with little honey-colored dots.

It was all he could do to stop himself from lowering his lips to a small scar he saw there. He'd been celibate a long time, but he hadn't realized it had been *this* long.

"Are you hungry, Constance?" he asked briskly.

He saw her blink once. "Famished," she replied.

"Then come with me." He tucked her arm into his and walked her toward the buffet table in the dining room. He handed her a plate.

The spread was impressive. There were large succulent prawns on ice, fancy meat and pastry roll-ups, several fruit salads, vegetable sticks and luscious chocolates.

While she pondered the table, he went into the kitchen to snatch two glasses and open a bottle of champagne. He returned to find her plate holding a very modest amount of shrimp and raw vegetables.

He led the way back to the stairs, walked halfway up, then settled them comfortably on a carpeted stair, letting his legs stretch down to make room for hers.

"Tell me, Constance," he said, placing the glass on the stair and pouring champagne, "Are you a member of the historical society?"

She bit a shrimp in half, then shook her head as she chewed. "No. But I'm glad I happened to be here for the party."

"You don't live in Dancer's Beach?"

"I'm…visiting."

"Family?"

"Friends."

"Friends are important," he said. "I value mine."

She nodded. "The other two Musketeers?"

He laughed. "You noticed. I guess the costumes are corny, but we saw them and sort of related, I guess."

"To the fight against despotic evil?"

"Nothing so noble," he denied candidly. "To the camaraderie, the tankards of ale, the wenching."

She tsked. "Wenching isn't healthy."

"Yeah, well, like a lot of men, I talk more than I do."

He drank his champagne to cover his close observation of her as she admired the elegantly carved stairway. He was trying to imagine her without the mask.

"I don't recall that the Musketeers had such elegant surroundings," she said.

"Mmm." He refilled her glass, then his own. "When we're not Musketeering, we need someplace comfortable to be."

"But this is so big."

"I know. It needs children, parties."

"Do you have them?"

He smiled. "The children? No. No wife yet, either, but I'm looking."

"Ah." She took another bite of prawn. "The prospective Mrs. D'Artagnan might be here tonight." She pointed with her glass toward a very attractive woman dressed as Cleopatra. "The Queen of Egypt is very fetching."

He glanced at the woman, agreed with a nod, then turned back to his plate. "But there are all those palace intrigues and I understand she has something going with the Emperor of Rome. Are you single?"

She nodded absently, then asked, "Do you know anything about the history of this wonderful house?"

"Just a little," he replied. He didn't want to talk about the house, he wanted to talk about her. And him. "It was built before the turn of the century by someone who married into the Buckley family that founded Dancer's Beach."

"It's nice to have a house with history. Are you the owner?"

"I've just recently moved in with a couple of friends." All he could think about was how beautiful this woman was, even with half her face covered. "We're not very settled yet, but we're working on it."

"What do you do, Mr...?"

"D'Artagnan," he replied, liking the mystery. He didn't have to share his past, his fears, his regrets. "I'm a defender of France, a—"

She put a hand on his arm to stop him and he felt the small, sizzling jolt of it go right to his heart.

"No," she said seriously. "What do you really do?"

There was a subtle urgency in her voice that alerted him to something, he wasn't sure what.

But she smiled sweetly at him, and he decided it was the sudden rise in volume of the room's noise level. Too many years as a secret agent had left him with a certain paranoia that was difficult to shake.

The musicians had arrived and set up in the conservatory off the living room. Their tuning up rivaled the laughter and conversation of the hundred or so guests moving through the first floor.

A mellow mood settled over him and suddenly the last place he wanted to be with this woman was wedged on a stair in a room grown so loud that conversation was becoming difficult.

"Will you come upstairs with me?" he asked.

It wasn't until he saw the flash in her eyes, even behind the mask, that he realized how that abrupt question must have sounded.

"No, no, no," he assured her quickly. "I meant

upstairs to the sitting room. I can't even hear myself think down here."

She continued to look suspicious.

Oh, no, he thought. She'd been so warm and interested in what he had to say a moment ago. That careless question couldn't mean the end of what had seemed so promising.

He remembered her interest in the house—though he was suddenly having a little difficulty focusing on the details that might interest her—and said quickly, "And I have more to tell you."

"About what?" she asked a little stiffly.

"About the house. About...why I'm here."

She sat still for one more moment, then she picked up her plate and stood. "All right," she said. "I'd love to hear more."

AT LAST! Athena thought. The prospect of information she could use!

She preceded him up the stairs, then waited at the top for him to take the lead. He'd left the little reading alcove near the head of the stairs, she noticed, a half-moon-shaped spot where the railing looped out to look down on the floor below.

Her aunt's cane-seated rocker was gone, but in its place was a high-back leather chair and matching ottoman. The stained glass lamp depicting birds in flight, which she'd always admired as a child and had looked forward to sitting beside one day, stood nearby.

But D'Artagnan was moving along the corridor to a room at the far end. They passed several bedrooms on the way, but she knew that the sitting room he was heading for connected to the master bedroom.

His step was unsteady, she saw, as he changed course ever so slightly to avoid collision with the doorway. She wondered what accounted for that. He'd had several glasses of champagne while they were sitting on the stairs, but the glasses were small. He hadn't eaten, though, and champagne did have more of a kick than other types of alcohol.

There was a green futon where the gold brocade settee had been. Her aunt used to read them bedtime stories in this room when she and her sisters were very small, then they would all scamper off to their own bedrooms.

She put her plate on a low bamboo table and sat down.

He refilled their glasses, sat beside her on the futon, then raised his glass to hers. "To new discoveries," he said.

"Discoveries?" she questioned.

He clicked the rim of his glass to hers. "You. I've been looking for you."

She felt a moment's trepidation. Did he know her plan? He couldn't possibly. "You have? Why?"

He put a hand to the beaded headpiece that covered her hair and touched gently. "Because I need you," he whispered, suddenly urgent, intense. "Where...have you been?"

There was sincerity in what she could see of his eyes. Tenderness in his touch. Response rose in her, instinctive and as urgent as he sounded.

She put her glass down and reminded herself

sharply of why she was here. And that this could be
the man who'd coerced her aunt out of her home,
possibly even caused her death. At the very least, he
was one of Hartford's friends. She had to know more.

She took a prawn from her plate and put it to his
lips. "I think you need something to eat," she said.
"Come on. Take a bite."

He nipped the edge of the prawn with his teeth and
drew it into his mouth. "I don't remember these being
this good," he said, "until you touched them."

"You were going to tell me about the house." She
drank from her glass to encourage him to drink his,
on the principle of *in vino veritas*.

He obliged her. "It's a place," he said, his voice
very quiet as he concentrated on her, "for lots of
children. For visiting grandparents. For friends to
sleep over and for club meetings and loud Christmas
parties."

For a moment she couldn't reply. She'd always
thought that, too, but as long as she'd been coming
here, it had housed only Aunt Sadie and a cook-
housekeeper. She'd looked forward to herself and her
sisters and their families giving it the bursting-at-the-
seams hilarity it deserved.

But did *he* own it? Was he Hartford? "Then, it's
your home?" she asked.

He didn't seem to have heard her.

"I never had that," he went on. He took her glass
from her and put it with his on the table. He sloshed
a little and she reached forward instinctively to mop
up the liquid with a napkin, but he stopped her, catch-

ing her hand in his and leaning her back into his other arm.

"My house was empty. Of everything. Three times bigger than this but..." He sighed and closed his eyes for a moment. "No laughter. No music. No voices in the dark."

Athena was struck by that description. She could hear the silence he described. And for one surprisingly clear moment, could imagine a small boy alone in a big, dark house, surrounded by that silence.

She could feel his loneliness.

He tugged at her headpiece. "Can we take this off?" he asked.

She forced her mind away from him and back to what she was trying to do here. She pulled off the headpiece and let her hair fall.

"It's...beautiful," he said softly, pulling her into his arms and rubbing his cheek against it. She was beginning to lose her focus. She didn't want to know that he'd had an empty, lonely childhood. She didn't want to feel sympathy for this man.

She wanted to know if he owned the house, and if so, how he'd gotten it and whether or not he'd had anything to do with the plane crash that killed Sadie.

"D'Artagnan!" she said sharply, for want of his real name.

"Here, Constance," he said, falling onto his back and bringing her with him. "I'm yours." He held her face in both his hands and kissed her.

He smelled of toothpaste and champagne and an herbal aftershave. He was ardent and tender at the same time, and even in this slightly tipsy state, he was completely competent and masterful.

Then, while she was distracted by her own loss of equilibrium even though she was the sober one, he slipped up her mask and smiled as he looked into her face.

"I knew it," he whispered. "Beautiful. Beautiful." Then he winced, closed his eyes and muttered a quiet expletive.

She pushed up against his shoulders. "What?" she asked in concern.

He ran a hand over his face. "Allergy... medication," he said, shaking his head as though trying to clear it. "Champagne. Bad." He expelled a sigh as he held on to her with one hand, trying to sit up.

She tried to help by pulling on his arm but didn't have sufficient leverage. He caught a fistful of her slip, exposed by her awkward position, and tried to draw himself up with it, but the combination of medication and alcohol was too strong and he fell backward, ripping off a large piece of silk.

Athena punched his shoulder once. "Wake up!" she demanded. "I want to talk to you!"

His eyes opened languidly and he caught her fist and kissed it. Then he was out like a light.

She could have wept with frustration.

She reached for his mask, wanting at least to know what *he* looked like, sure that would help her somehow. But she heard voices on the other side of the door. And it wasn't locked.

She looked at the state of her costume, her host and

the fact that she wasn't even invited to this party, and decided that retreat was the wisest course of action.

At a knock on the door and a questioning "Hello?" she bolted, heading for the French doors that she knew led out to a veranda with stairs down to the backyard. Thanks to the rainy February night, the party would not have spilled outside.

She heard the sitting room door open when she was halfway down the stairs and ran through the darkness without looking back. She knew the way. She'd run down this road where she'd left the car a hundred times as a child.

But never with a man's kisses stinging her lips, and a piece of her slip still caught in his hand.

Chapter Three

September

Where did he go from here?

David reread the three paragraphs on his monitor for the sixth time.

> Jake stared moodily out the back window of the cab as it made the turn to Janie's bungalow. He hadn't had a letter in months, but then he hadn't written her, either. Life had been too hard, too dark to chronicle it for her.
>
> The cab pulled up in front of 722 Bramble Lane. Jake paid the driver and stepped out.
>
> Janie was sitting on the front steps with a cup of coffee and a book. She looked up at the slam of the car door, froze for a moment, then dropped the book and the coffee.

The cursor blinked at the indent on the next paragraph as he waited for inspiration.

She ran into his arms?

He ran into hers?

She walked inside and slammed the door?

Jake pounded on the door?

David hadn't a clue. He was writing the last chapter of his novel, trying to make his hero's personal dreams come true after the hell he'd put him through in the previous three hundred pages.

But David couldn't guess how Janie would react after she'd been skillfully wooed, willingly seduced, then left to fend for herself while Jake answered the CIA's call after assuring her he was through with the work.

As he'd done at least once a day for months, he thought back to the costume party last February, and the woman who'd appeared in his living room like the realization of a dream.

He remembered her smile, the shape of her chin, snippets of their conversation. There were gaps in his memories. The champagne, the antihistamine and only four hours of sleep the night before had combined to knock him on his butt, but he recalled one crystal clear glimpse of her.

A heart-shaped face. Eyes the color of his favorite chambray shirt. A smile that tripped his pulse. And breasts that spilled out of her Empress Josephine dress like exotic blooms.

He could close his eyes now and catch the rose-and-spice scent of her that had clung to him when he'd awakened in the sitting room. He'd been alone on the futon with part of her slip caught in his fist and the taste of her on his lips.

He couldn't remember what had happened, but he could imagine. The first few minutes of their meeting were clear in his memory—and he'd been plotting her seduction since then.

He remembered taking her upstairs, pouring more champagne, taking her in his arms and...had he told her about his lonely childhood, or had he just dreamed that? He couldn't be sure.

But he wished he could be sure he hadn't hurt her, offended her, upset her.

He'd tried to find her, but without a name or any idea what she did or who the friends were she was visiting, it had been impossible.

Even Mrs. Beasley hadn't known who she was, though she remembered the dress. She'd arrived with friends, she said, and that was all she knew.

David got up from the computer and went downstairs to the kitchen to pour a cup of coffee and read the editorial page and his horoscope. He forced himself to write three pages every morning before allowing himself that luxury. Otherwise, he'd find a dozen excuses to keep him from the computer.

He'd submitted a full synopsis and three chapters of the novel to an agent in New York, primarily as a way to make himself finish it.

Writing columns, though putting him under the stress of three weekly deadlines, had been easy compared to writing fiction. And in a way, his work as a government agent had been the same. He'd had a clear subject, his own observations and feelings to draw from, input from other people.

In writing fiction, he sat there all alone, except for the demanding blink of the cursor. There were no source materials. Everything came out of his heart or his head and usually lived there behind closed doors, resisting his every effort to force them open.

When the doors did open, the material came at him haphazardly. It made him hurt, made him laugh, made him angry, made him wish he'd chosen to do anything but be a writer.

Until he put just the right words together and made a nebulous thought clear in a beautiful way. And then it was all right. He was all right.

But every morning was a fresh struggle. Every day he had to figure out just how he'd done it the day before.

He poured some Colombian roast into a plain brown mug and carried it to the living room coffee table where he'd left the paper.

He turned on the television for the noise. Dotty, his housekeeper, was away for a few days, Trevyn was somewhere in a remote spot of the Canadian mountains, taking pictures for a calendar, a commission he earned every year. With Bram in Mexico on a case for his already thriving detective agency, Cliffside was quiet as a tomb.

He folded back the editorial page as the weather report promised another week of Indian summer for the Oregon coast. Then the newscaster's voice said, "We'll show this item one more time for those of you who are joining us late or missed last night's report. This woman was found in the Columbia River off Astoria by a pilot boat. She's in fair condition at Columbia Memorial Hospital in Astoria, but cannot remember her name, where she lives, or how she

ended up in the water. The Coast Guard reported no
capsized boats or distress calls.''

David looked up from the paper, his attention
snagged by the story—and felt his heart stall in his
chest. He got up, knocked over his coffee in the process and stood stock-still in shock.

The grainy photo of the woman remained on the
screen while the newscaster pleaded for anyone who
knew this woman to contact the Astoria police.

The photo showed a woman on a stretcher, long
red hair wet and lank against the pillow, her eyes
closed. Her features were difficult to distinguish, but
he knew the shape of that face, the delicate point of
the chin. It was Constance! And her stomach
mounded up under the blanket covering her, clearly
in a very advanced state of pregnancy.

His heart hammered its way into his throat. Oh,
God.

In his fuzzy memories of that February night, he
saw her lying atop him, her hair free of the confining
headpiece. He'd been filled with lust for her and she'd
been so warm and responsive.

Though he struggled to remember, he still couldn't
recall what had happened after that.

Until he awakened later that night with part of her
slip in his hands and her scent clinging to him.

''If anyone has *any* information about this woman,
please call the Astoria police.''

After all this time! After all his efforts to find out
who she was! Pregnant and with amnesia?

He tucked the pad under his arm, grabbed his keys,
his cell phone and his jacket as he raced out to the

garage. He climbed into the silver-blue sedan between Trevyn's truck and Bram's Jeep and dialed the number from the broadcast before racing down the road to the highway.

His conversation with the officer to whom his call was transferred was surreal.

"I'm calling about the young woman fished out of the Columbia River last night," he said, trying to sound calm rather than the way he really felt.

"Your name, sir?"

"David Hartford from Dancer's Beach. Is she all right?" he demanded.

"I believe so. You know who she is?"

"Yes." He knew who she was. She had walked out of his dreams, lived in his heart.

"And what's her name?"

"I…ah…don't know."

"But I thought you knew her."

"I do. She came to a party at my home. But we were all wearing…masks." It wasn't until he got to the last word in his explanation that he realized what this must sound like to the officer. "It was a fund-raiser," he added lamely, "for the historical society."

"I see. And she didn't tell you her name?"

"No, I was dressed as a Musketeer and she…" He could feel his credibility diminishing. "No, she didn't."

"I see. Then, how do you feel you can help?"

He hadn't really considered that. He'd just wanted to see her. "I can take care of her," he said, "until you find out who she is."

"We can't release her into your custody, sir, if you're not a relative."

"But you don't have a relative if you don't know who she is! What'll become of her when she's ready to leave the hospital?"

David was at the highway now and had to concentrate to turn into the morning rush-hour traffic.

Fortunately the officer didn't have an answer for that until David was comfortably ensconced in the stream of cars driving north.

"I'll have to look into that for you, sir."

"Thank you," David said. "I'll be there in three hours."

"It's a long drive from Dancer's Beach, sir. Take your time. We'll be here."

ATHENA SAT IN THE BACK of a cab taking her from the Astoria Airport at the Coast Guard Air Station to Columbia Memorial Hospital. She folded her arms against the need to hold on to the front seat and shout "Faster! Faster!"

She couldn't believe that she'd seen her sister on the news, pale and limp and pregnant, dragged out of a river like an old boot. She couldn't imagine what had happened.

And she wasn't entirely sure which sister this was. She and Alexis and Augusta talked on the telephone once a week, but she hadn't seen either of them since their masquerade party fiasco in February. They'd met up again at the car that night as planned, both Lex and Gusty convinced that the Musketeers could not have been involved in anything illegal.

''He was too considerate,'' worldly Lex had insisted of her Musketeer.

''Too…sweet,'' Gusty had sighed.

The following day, they'd all returned home and Athena had spent the next month determined to find incriminating information on David Hartford. She'd hounded Patrick until he'd used every last source he knew, and still his results were unsatisfactory. He could find nothing on Hartford or his friends to take to the police.

''Hartford seems to be a paragon of virtue and journalistic skill, Bishop was decorated several times in the army, and McGinty was simply a drifter when he wasn't taking brilliant pictures.''

''But what about the gaps in time you can't account for?'' she'd asked.

He'd sighed. ''I've done everything, Athena. It's just not there.''

''But how can that be? I thought with all our information on the Internet, everyone's life story was vulnerable to everyone else's scrutiny.''

''I don't know. I'll keep looking, but be prepared for it to take a while.''

That had been seven months ago.

Athena was trying to accept the situation, to convince herself that their aunt had left the house to Hartford just because she'd wanted to.

And then she'd watched the ten-o'clock news while on her treadmill and stared at her sister's face on television. But the photo was grainy, though a very distinct pregnancy was clear. She'd heard her own little cry of surprise.

She'd called Gusty and gotten no answer. And there was no one at the school at that hour.

Then she'd called Lex in Rome and the message on her answering machine said—in English and in Italian—that she was off on a sketching trip to try to reinspire herself and would be out of touch for a week. Alexis, in a creative mode, always sought privacy.

So, who'd been pulled out of the river? The picture had been so unclear, and even under good conditions she and her sisters could misidentify one another from a distance.

And what on earth had whoever-it-was been doing in Astoria, Oregon? And pregnant?

Athena had called the hospital to say she was the sister of the mystery woman, and canceled the next few days' appointments. She'd taken the red eye to Portland, then an early-morning commuter flight from Portland to Astoria.

She had no love life, she told herself, but she had a family life that was complicated enough to keep four people busy.

The cab pulled up to the covered main entrance of the hospital. Athena paid the driver, then leaped out while he retrieved her bag from the trunk. She ran to the main desk, told the clerk who she was, and was treated to one startled moment of staring.

"We've been expecting you, Miss Ames," the clerk said, then called someone. A policeman appeared a moment later. He was tall and slender and probably in his late thirties. "Officer Holden," he said, hands resting on the creaky leather of his belt. "Would you come with me, please?"

"I'll watch your bag," the clerk promised.

Athena handed it over the counter.

"It'll be right back here when you return."

"Is my sister okay?" Athena asked the officer as she followed him. "Last night's news report said she was in satisfactory condition."

"She...was fine when the nurse looked in on her at 6:12 a.m.," he replied, a little evasively, Athena thought.

"You say that as though you think her condition might have changed," she said as she chased his long steps down the hall.

"Well, I think what's happened suggests that she was feeling much better."

"What do you mean? What's happened?"

He pushed open the door to Room 115. Inside was an empty, unmade bed.

"She seems to have run away," Officer Holden said.

Athena stared at the empty room, sunshine streaming in through the window and across the rumpled bedclothes, and felt her heart sink like an anchor.

"You must be her twin," the officer said. "I spoke to her briefly last night, and though she looked a little the worse for her experience—you're identical."

Athena heard the question though her brain wasn't focused enough to process an answer. She felt herself nod—yes, they were identical—but her mind was occupied with more important questions about what had happened. Why did she leave? Where would she go? And who was it—Gusty or Lex?

And the most nagging question if not the most important—who'd fathered her sister's baby, and why hadn't she told her sisters about it?

Then she heard a man's voice speaking to Officer Holden and looked up, thinking it was the doctor.

But it wasn't. This man wore jeans and a gray cotton sweater. He looked grim until he caught sight of her, then a smile smoothed the worry lines on his forehead. He came toward her and caught her arms, his grip firm as he pulled her to him. "You're all right!" he said, wrapping his arms around her. "You looked so pale and weak on television, I thought..."

She stood in limp surprise in his arms, then he stiffened suddenly and held her away from him. A new frown appeared between his eyes as he looked her over. "You're not pregnant," he said in what sounded like confusion.

He looked into her eyes and she felt the contact like a physical touch somewhere deep inside where she already felt lost. "I don't understand."

Frankly, neither did she.

"Miss Ames," the officer said, "this is David Hartford, an acquaintance of your sister. Mr. Hartford, Athena Ames, our mystery woman's twin."

Hartford! The name reverberated in her brain while she forced a polite smile and shook his hand. The Musketeer who owned Sadie's house!

"But where's the woman from the river?" he asked the officer.

Holden pointed to the empty bed. "Gone. I'm sorry."

Athena's attention was suddenly divided between correcting the officer about being a twin, and complete surprise that one of the Musketeers was here to find Gusty. "How did you know her?" she asked the stranger.

He shifted and put a hand to the foot of the bed. He had dark hair and eyes and a lean but powerful body that seemed all shoulders and upper arms.

"I didn't know her that well," he said, and she got the impression he regretted that. "But I recognized her. She was at a party at my home last February."

She had to sit on the side of the bed before her knees gave way. "I...I can't imagine what's happened to her," she said, her brain working feverishly to figure out how a party in Dancer's Beach at a house that was left to this stranger by her aunt was connected to a small town one hundred and fifty miles up the coast, where her sister had been fished out of the river. And why had that drawn David Hartford?

Could this possibly get any more confusing? Or make less sense? She didn't think so.

"What do you mean gone?" David Hartford demanded of the officer. "How can an ill woman simply walk out of a hospital without being stopped?"

Holden shrugged. "They figure she did it while they were busy dispensing medications or serving breakfasts."

"So a woman who doesn't know who she is, where she comes from, or where to go is just wandering the street?"

"We've asked the television station to keep running the photo. And we'll give it to the newspaper. At least now we know who she is." He looked though a small notebook he carried. "Can I have her first name, Miss Ames?"

Athena made a quick decision she prayed would not further confound the situation. She couldn't say, "It's either Alexis or Augusta," because the officer had just told Hartford she was a twin, not a triplet.

And while that could be easily corrected, she didn't know what Hartford's involvement was in all this, and having a third sister he didn't know about might work to her advantage.

So on the shaky conclusion that Lex was still in Europe somewhere and had simply taken off on one of her art trips, and that Gusty usually checked in once a week but hadn't this week, she replied, "Augusta. Augusta Amelia Ames."

"Her age?" He smiled when she hesitated. "We're gentlemen here. We'll forget that it reveals yours, also."

"Twenty-nine," she said. "Five foot seven, about one hundred twenty-two pounds—except, of course, for the pregnancy."

"Any idea where she might have gone?"

Athena shook her head. "She lives north of Sacramento, California in a town called Pansy Junction. She teaches school there. I have no idea what she was even doing here."

"Any guesses where she might go?"

"None. Unless she's trying to go home. But if she

doesn't remember who she is, she won't know where that is—so I guess that doesn't make sense, does it?''

Hartford put a hand on her shoulder. Its warmth and gentleness surprised her.

A tall man in a lab coat over jeans walked into the room. He was bald and wore glasses and a reluctant expression. A name badge on his lapel said he was Dr. Stoddard.

He stopped several feet inside the door when he saw Athena, a shocked expression on his face.

''This is your patient's twin, Doctor,'' Holden said. ''Miss Ames, this is Dr. Stoddard, who treated your sister last night.''

The doctor shook his head in amazement. ''You're identical,'' he observed.

She nodded.

He sat beside her. ''I'm sorry,'' he said. ''I've spoken to everyone on duty this morning, and no one saw her leave. Mornings are a very busy time for us.''

''But why would she leave,'' Athena asked, distress gaining control of her efforts to remain calm, ''if she didn't know where to go from here?''

''Agitation, I would guess,'' he replied. ''She had a blow to her forehead that probably caused the amnesia. I've never dealt with anything like this myself, but I did a little research last night and found that often a patient's tendency is to run in such circumstances. If she woke up headachy and unable to come up with any answers about herself or her situation, she probably thought she could find the answers…somewhere.''

Athena asked one of the questions that had plagued

her for the entire flight across country. "Doctor, did my sister say anything to you about the baby's father?"

"No, she didn't," he replied. "If she doesn't know who *she* is, she probably doesn't remember her husband, either. Or her boyfriend."

"You don't know who he is?" Holden asked, making notes on a small pad.

She spread her hands helplessly. "I didn't even know she was pregnant." She focused on the doctor and reluctantly asked her second question. "Do you think her being in the water was the result of an accident, or that she was struck or pushed or something?"

The doctor shrugged. "Hard to say. The blow might have been consistent with striking the steering wheel. She might have gone off the bridge in a car."

"But there was no sign of a crash along the guardrail on the Young's Bay Bridge," Holden said. "And, of course, she wouldn't have survived a fall off the Astoria-Megler Bridge."

Athena frowned in question.

"The big bridge to Washington," he explained. "And so far, we haven't found a car, but that doesn't mean it isn't in the river, somewhere. She was recovered in the dark at high tide."

Dr. Stoddard was paged over the public address system. He stood. "I have to answer that page, Miss Ames. I'm sorry about your sister, but she's in generally good health, except for the amnesia. And the Astoria police are very good at their jobs. They'll find her."

"What about the baby?" Athena asked.

He nodded. "Also in good shape. An obstetrician looked her over, and despite what she'd been through, the baby was fine. She's about twenty-nine weeks along."

Holden walked her and David Hartford out into the hallway. "We'll do our best, Miss Ames. We'll keep running that photo on the news, and we'll give it to all our officers and the state police so there'll be someone on the lookout up and down the coast."

Athena nodded. It seemed a pitiful solution when she thought of her sister all alone, lost in a void where she had no name, no past, and no connection to anyone in the present.

She just hoped to God that Gusty had a future.

If it *was* Gusty.

"Where will you be if I have information," Holden asked, "or more questions?"

Athena was momentarily at a loss. "Right now, I'm not sure," she said. "I came straight here in a cab from the airport. And I'm not sure I'll get a motel. I may just rent a car and drive around looking for Gusty myself. But you can call me on my cell phone." She gave him the number.

"This isn't the best time to be visiting Astoria," the officer said. "Motel rooms are full up because of the Fish Festival. And my guess is you won't be able to find a car, either." He turned to Hartford. "And where can I reach you?"

Hartford gave him an address and a phone number.

Holden closed and pocketed his book. "All right. Think positive and I'll get back to you when I can."

Athena retraced the path down which Holden had led her, retrieved her bag from the smiling clerk, then pushed her way through the revolving doors, Hartford right behind her.

She stood on the pavement in front of the hospital. "What do I do now if I can't rent a car or find a room?" she wondered out loud in a mild panic.

"I have a thought," David Hartford said.

HIS IDEA WAS CRAZY, David told himself, and would probably send her running in the opposite direction, convinced he was a lunatic with designs on her body, but it just might be an efficient solution to her problem. And she looked too much like his "Constance" to just abandon her to her own devices.

She looked at him warily. "Yes?"

"My home is halfway down the coast," he said, trying to sound calm and reasonable. He didn't feel those things. The mystery woman he'd spent the night with and made a baby with, was wandering around lost in an unfamiliar place, cold and lonely and probably terrified. "Why don't we drive down the coast together. We'll check out all the little towns in between, and you can stay with me until we hear something. We'll be better as a search team than we would be separately."

That earned him precisely the look he'd expected. So he explained.

"She's carrying my baby," he said.

Her eyes grew enormous and her mouth fell open. "You're the boyfriend?"

"Not exactly, but I have a lot invested here, too. You're safe with me, I promise you."

She stammered but he kept talking.

"I have a very big house with six bedrooms. I have an office at one end of the upstairs, and you can have the room farthest away from it, if you like. I can also provide you with a car."

"Why didn't you tell Officer Holden it's your baby?" she challenged suspiciously.

That was a tough one. "Because," he admitted, "the details are sketchy."

"I don't understand."

"I'll explain when we get to Cliffside. That's where I live. In Dancer's Beach."

She was caving; he could tell. Her pointed chin identical to Constance's—Augusta's—softened and her tight jaw relaxed.

"That's a big house," she said, "for a single man."

"I like the space," he said. "A couple of friends also live on the property, but they're out of town at the moment."

"Convenient," she said.

"Fact," he corrected.

She looked into his eyes and there was something so familiar about the way her gaze bored into him— but, then, of course it would be familiar. She was Con...Augusta's twin.

"All right," she said. "But I warn you. I'm a lawyer. You do anything I don't like, and before you even know what happened, I'll own everything you have."

He grinned and took her bag. "That's what I like. A shy, retiring woman. Come on. I'm the blue sedan."

She settled into the plush passenger seat as he stowed her bag in the back, then climbed in behind the wheel.

"This is very elegant," she said, running a hand over the blue glove leather. "Six-bedroom house, pricey car with real leather upholstery. Are *you* a doctor?"

"No, I'm a writer."

"A journalist?"

"Used to be. Now I write fiction."

"Really. I hope it's murder mysteries so that you're blessed with good investigative skills that'll find Gusty."

"Gusty?"

"Augusta." She frowned at him. "The woman who's pregnant with your baby. How did that happen, anyway?"

Preparing to back out of his parking space, he turned to her instead, an eyebrow raised ironically. "I didn't know her name. And I don't really have to explain about how babies are made, do I?"

She pursed her lips at him. The gesture was distracting. It was going to be hard to remember that she was Augusta's twin and not the woman herself.

"I meant how did it all get so—" she was backpedaling, her hands making a wide gesture to replace the words she seemed to feel obliged to avoid "—intimate," she finally said. "When you didn't even know her name."

"It was a costume party," he replied. "We were wearing masks."

"And that prevented you from introducing yourselves to each other?"

"No." He backed out of the spot and headed for the exit on a street that ran parallel to the highway. "But it made it easier to pretend to be other people."

Gusty had made love with David Hartford? What on earth had happened that night to make her usually shy sister so forthcoming?

Athena tried to imagine Gusty making love to a stranger and couldn't. But she had. Or maybe it was Lex who had. That would be more believable.

Whoever it had been had obviously found the costumes and the feigned identities more conducive to romance. Or she'd gone much too far in her efforts to make her Musketeer talk.

"That doesn't sound like Gusty," she said. "She's shy and gentle. A real nurturer. I can't imagine her getting entangled in a fantasy."

"Well, that's because you're her sister." He followed the street to the first traffic light, then headed for the highway. He turned onto a one-way street that led to the downtown area. "Even though you're her twin, I'm sure there are things she doesn't tell you. Everyone has a private place no one else knows about. Qualities we keep to ourselves. She was sweet, but she was also saucy and seductive."

"Saucy?" she asked in surprise. Her eyes were scanning the sidewalk for any sign that her sister might still be nearby, but that remark brought her eyes to his face. "You're kidding? Seductive?"

He shook his head and she got the impression that, though the time he'd spent with Gusty had been brief, he felt as though he knew her well.

That was an understatement, she thought wryly, considering Gusty was seven months' pregnant.

"I thought so," he replied. "But, then, she'd seemed as eager as I was and I guess I was egocentric enough to like that. She was the most wonderful woman I've ever met."

His eyes scanned the left side of the highway as he watched for her.

Was he talking about Lex, Athena wondered? Gusty was wonderful, but saucy and seductive simply did not describe her.

Lex, on the other hand, was a skilled vamp. She used her talents carefully, but Athena had seen her in action and she was remarkable. But she'd have been prepared against pregnancy, wouldn't she?

Athena suddenly realized how she could determine which of her sisters he'd made love to.

"What kind of costume was she wearing?" she asked conversationally. To herself, she asked, *Flapper, or Southern belle?*

"I'm not sure what you'd call it," he said, frowning at the road. "It was high-waisted with short, puffy sleeves. It looked like something Napoleon's Josephine would have worn."

It was all Athena could do to withhold the gasp of shock and utter confusion she felt at that reply.

David Hartford was *her* Musketeer!

Chapter Four

Athena didn't know which discrepancy in his story to focus on first—the fact that he'd considered *her* saucy and seductive, or his seemingly sincere conviction that he'd gotten her pregnant!

Saucy and seductive. She found herself smiling while still scanning the bustling passersby. Her?

She'd never thought of herself in those terms, and was certain no one else ever had—including the men she'd dated. She'd always been the scrapper, the one who defended her sisters against insult or injury.

As an adult, she'd gone to war for the little guy, and she'd finally opened her own law firm because she got tired of superiors telling her to stick to cases she could win—and which ones those were.

She'd built a formidable reputation as a courtroom bulldog. Hardly a saucy or seductive image.

It was true that she had tried to turn on the charm the night of the costume party, but to think that it had actually worked amazed her.

And what was it he had said earlier? Her pulse picked up its beat as she remembered the words. "She was the most wonderful woman I've ever met."

Everything she was so worried about faded into the background for one brief moment as she basked in the unfamiliar glory of that title.

Then she remembered that she wasn't the important issue here, her sister was—and she *still* didn't know which sister. She had to find an opportunity to call the Pansy Junction school again.

But why did David think he was the father?

"So," she began carefully, "the two of you had a wildly romantic evening?"

He glanced away from the road for a moment and toward her, a pleat between his eyebrows. "Apparently."

"You're not sure?"

He shrugged as he focused on the road. "I'd been taking antihistamines and we were drinking champagne and I guess I passed out. When I woke up, I had part of her slip in my hand and..."

He had turned the car up a quiet side street, his frown deepening.

"Her scent was on my shirt," he said. "On my hands. Roses with something spicy mixed in."

Something melted inside her at the reverent way he said that.

"Then, you don't actually remember?"

He smiled and put a hand to his heart. "In here I do. I can't explain it."

She could only stare at him, but he didn't notice. He'd turned again and was driving on the main downtown street, another one-way in the opposite direction, and he was looking over every pedestrian carefully.

"The nurse noticed she was missing," he said, "when she brought her breakfast. If she hasn't eaten, she might stop in somewhere for coffee or a donut."

"But she doesn't have any money. At least, I don't think she does. She had no purse, nothing, when she was pulled out of the water."

He turned into a parking spot in front of the Danish Maid Bakery. "It's worth a look. Have you eaten?"

"No." She unbuckled her belt, prepared to follow him. "I had peanuts on the flight from Chicago to Portland."

"I'll treat you."

The bakery was a small, warm hub of activity. Four booths were filled with people for whom this appeared to be a morning routine: joggers ending their runs with coffee and a muffin, and men and women dressed for business starting the day with something sweet.

But there was no sign of Gusty. They emerged with paper cups of coffee. Athena nibbled on a buttermilk bar, and David downed a Bismarck in several bites.

They looked into a small diner right off the main street, the Brown Bagger Deli farther up Commercial, then Andrew and Steve's down another block.

They emerged from their last stop with nothing more than second cups of coffee and disappointment.

Hartford studied her grim expression. "I'm sorry," he said as they stood on the sidewalk. "I can only imagine how worried you must be, but we'll find her."

"I know." She tried to sound as convinced as he did. "I just want it to be now. Today."

She couldn't shake the image of Gusty—who hadn't wanted anything to do with the costume party plan in the first place—now lost and alone and very pregnant.

Ensnared by the image, Athena stepped off the curb, starting back in the direction of the car as she sipped at her covered coffee cup.

There was a shout from behind her, the blare of a horn, and then a strong hand on her arm snatched her back as a beat-up pickup sped past, horn still honking.

"Whoa," David said, looking her over for signs of injury. "It isn't going to do anyone any good if in finding Augusta, we lose you in the process. You all right?"

She wasn't. Her heart was in her throat and she was trembling. She'd started something bad at the costume party that now seemed to be generating its own ill wind.

One of her sisters was pregnant and missing. David Hartford thought he'd impregnated her, but he hadn't. And he thought *she* was Gusty. Or was it Lex?

"I'm fine," she lied.

He studied her another minute, then took her arm and after waiting for a break between cars, led her across the street.

"You have to relax." He let his hand fall when they reached the sidewalk. "The tension will snap you in half. I know you're worried and upset, but you can't help your sister if you're not thinking straight."

"I just…feel responsible." The words were risky, but she couldn't stop them from coming out. She'd always been honest as a child, and studying the law and living by its mandates as an adult had made her even more scrupulous.

Although, she thought darkly, it would be hard to tell, considering her present circumstances. Her suspicions about Hartford had led her to uncharacteristically reckless behavior.

"Why?" he asked. "You didn't push her in the river."

No, but I forced her to pretend to be someone she wasn't and go to the party.

"I've just always felt like the oldest," she said, trying to explain.

"But you're twins."

"I was born thirty-seven minutes before she was. She's the gentle one, and I'm…"

He nodded. "The warrior. Your parents must have seen it, too, if they named you Athena."

"Maybe." She didn't want to talk about her parents. She had enough to think about already. "Does being a writer make you the expert on surviving tension?"

He laughed lightly. She liked the sound of it and what it did to his face on this morning that had been so much about bad news.

"Deadlines certainly would," he said as they walked a block toward Commercial Street. "But I've been in other kinds of situations, and you have to learn to control stress before it takes you over."

"What kind of situations?" she asked. Pursuing that line of thought was less worrisome than Gusty, so she followed it as they rounded the corner.

"Ah, investigations," he replied. Carefully, she thought.

She stopped in the middle of the sidewalk. "You mean you're a detective?"

"Sort of," he said, walking on. She followed.

"How can you be sort of a detective?"

"Well, before I turned to fiction writing, I did a column for the *Chicago Tribune*. A little social observation, a little investigative reporting about what was going on in town. It's sort of like detective work."

"Oh," she said flatly, disappointed. "I thought for a minute there that you were going to be able to call out a force of secret agents to help us."

He raised an eyebrow at that remark. He looked away for a moment and then replied, "Actually, one of my friends who lives in an apartment above my garage is a detective. I've been trying to reach him for advice, but I can't get through. He's working in Mexico."

Probably the former cop, she speculated, and not the photographer.

They'd reached the car and he unlocked it with the remote, then opened her door.

"So, what brought you to Oregon?" she asked conversationally.

"My friends and I were all at a kind of crossroads. Career changes. Life-style changes." He saw her in and closed her door, then walked around the car and slipped in behind the wheel. "We were looking for something new, I guess."

Escape from the law? she wondered. A decision to go straight when the law got too close?

"A friend left me the house where I'll be taking you." He sighed grimly. "It was a blessing for Bram and Trevyn and me—as though she'd reached down from heaven and handed us a wonderful gift. Even so, we'd all prefer she was still alive." He pointed uphill and away from the river. "We'll prowl another couple of streets, then we'll head down the coast."

He tried to put an end to the conversation, but she ignored him.

"She?" Athena asked in an even tone of voice so that he wouldn't suspect she knew the identity of his "friend." "A *girlfriend?*"

He drove in the direction he'd pointed. "No," he replied, his concentration focused on the occasional pedestrian. "A...sort of co-worker."

A co-worker? Sadie had been someone he knew while disappearing for months at a time? Or did he mean in his newspaper work?

No, he couldn't. Patrick said he'd worked on the *Chicago Tribune* since '91 and Sadie had lived in Dancer's Beach since the sixties.

So his acquaintance with Sadie had to have been during the times Patrick said he and his friends disappeared.

Or David was lying. And that, Athena thought, was the more likely explanation.

Athena decided that speculation was distracting her from the search for Gusty, so she pushed her thought away and focused on David's street-by-street search.

They'd scoured Seaside with its boardwalk atmosphere, then the artistic community of Cannon Beach before they talked again.

It was the middle of the afternoon, and they settled into a quiet corner table in a restaurant that resembled a large and very elegant log cabin. Athena rubbed at her forehead as she read the menu.

"Headache?" David asked.

"Sometimes after a long day," she said, massaging at her temples, "it just hurts to have my hair up."

"Can't you take it down?" he asked.

"It's not very tidy. I do it only on weekends."

He looked surprised, then indicated their surroundings. "No courtroom decorum required here. And isn't that jacket uncomfortable? And those heels?"

She shrugged and smiled tiredly. "It's lawyer gear. I'm used to them."

"There's the rest room. You can change if you brought something more comfortable with you."

It would be an opportunity to call the school.

"We still have a couple of hours' drive home," he encouraged.

Distracted she considered that. "If Gusty's walking, we've passed her up, haven't we?"

He nodded. "Or if she's somehow gotten transportation, she could be way ahead of us. It's hard to know. Maybe something drew her to Dancer's Beach."

"You mean because of you?"

He shook his head. "I'd like to think that, but I mean because she told me she had friends there. She came with them to the party. Do you know who they are?"

Dangerous ground. She'd made up the friends the night of the party to explain her presence there. She proceeded cautiously. "No, I don't. She didn't tell you who they are?"

He shook his head. "Mrs. Beasley saw her arrive with them, but didn't know who they were. I asked her the day after the party when I knew I had to find your sister again."

"You did?"

"Yeah. But I had no luck. Until that newscast this morning. I checked with the chamber of commerce because Mayor Beasley seemed to think her friends worked there, but apparently the costumes tricked her, too. The women at the chamber of commerce hadn't even come to the party." He sighed dispiritedly and Athena saw an unnamed emotion in his eyes before he turned them to his menu. "Tell me what you want," he said, "and I'll order for you while you're changing."

She did that, then hurried out to the car. She got the school's number out of her purse, then dug through her luggage while waiting for an answer.

No, Gusty had not reported to school that morning and could not be reached at home, according to a concerned secretary.

Athena passed on what information she had, then left her phone number and asked the woman to call her if Gusty reported in. Then she carried her clothes into the restaurant's ladies' room to change, trying to find comfort in the fact that now she at least knew who was missing.

DAVID WAS SHOCKED anew by Athena's beauty when she sat down again after putting on a pale blue knit sweater and slacks that he guessed was as close to casual as she ever got. Her hair was long and straight and parted in the middle, a yard of flaming silk down her back.

She flipped it over her shoulder before tucking eagerly into a turkey sandwich.

He couldn't believe how much she looked like Augusta. He'd known twins before, but he guessed he'd never seen identicals. It was uncanny. Unsettling.

"Did you and Augusta play tricks on people when you were children?" he asked. "You know—pretending to be each other?"

An instant blush filled her cheeks. Had he guessed?

But he laughed, apparently nothing in mind but that simple question. "I take it that's a yes?"

"A couple of times when we were in grade school," she said, remembering their antics with a smile. "I took Gusty's math test, and she gave my social studies report." Lex had taken the art test for both of them, but David didn't know about Lex yet.

"When we got older," she went on, "she landed the role of one of the pink ladies in *Grease,* but I went on for her one night because her boyfriend had broken up with her. He was in the play, too."

"How'd you do?"

"Not too badly. But she didn't speak to me for a week, because after the play, her boyfriend told me he was sorry for everything, and he wanted me back. I punched him in the nose, and I was kicked out of the drama club—or Gusty was."

He nodded as though he understood. "Your warrior nature at work again."

"I guess so. She forgave me eventually." She sobered suddenly as she wondered if she would ever forgive her for this.

"How did your parents tell you apart?" he asked. "I can't imagine trying to guide and discipline children if you're confused about who's who."

She shrugged, knowing they'd have to get to this sooner or later. People talked about themselves—that's how they got acquainted. And he was convinced he was Gusty's baby's father—he wanted to know about her life.

"Actually," she said with a sigh, "that was never much of a problem. Our father was a nice guy, but traveled all the time. He played professional baseball. Off season he did celebrity endorsements, cut ribbons, gave speeches, that sort of thing."

He listened attentively.

"Our mother and her sister," she went on, "had been very spoiled and beautiful children. Our father adored my mother and spoiled her, too—until we came along. Then he adored and spoiled us and she resented that."

"I'm sorry," he said gently.

"It doesn't matter anymore." She paused for a sip of coffee to help swallow the bitter disappointment that she'd never been able to fix the problem between her mother and her. "They're both gone now. They were going to a party in my dad's Corvette when I was in college and were hit at an intersection."

"It always matters." He reached for the coffee carafe and refilled her cup. "We carry the baggage of an unhappy childhood forever. And somehow death exaggerates the problem rather than solves it because you lose the chance to make it better."

She stared at him, astonished that he understood that.

"The three of—" She stopped abruptly. His insightful observation had made her drop her guard. "Gusty and I," she corrected smoothly, "had each other and that helped a lot. I think our mother tried to do her best by us for appearance sake, but we knew she considered us nuisances—and inferior ones at that. And Dad just stayed away because it was easier."

David shook his head, his expression empathetic. "And I always thought my family was dysfunctional. It makes my childhood sound like paradise."

"You listened to me," she said. "I'd be happy to return the favor."

He absently dipped a French fry into a dollop of ketchup. "My mother and yours might have been separated at birth. Except that mine had wealth rather than beauty, and that was always the focus of her attention. My dad was fun, but he died when I was nine, and my mother went through a long series of boyfriends and several other husbands after that. I was usually forgotten in the process. Fortunately, the household staff looked out for me."

Now it was Athena's turn to frown. That sounded even more unstable than her life had been. "Any siblings?"

"Yes," he replied. "Two little half brothers, ten

and twelve. They usually spend holidays and summers with me. They're up against the same things I was.''

''I guess,'' she said, trying to put a positive spin on what he'd told her, ''your experiences will give you a lot to write about.''

He nodded. ''What does it do for you?''

''I'm a defense attorney,'' she said, ''I just do my best to go to bat for the little guy.''

''What does Gusty do?'' he asked.

She felt inexplicably, unjustifiably jealous of his interest in Gusty. Particularly because she was the sweet one, the gentle one—the kind of woman who would appeal to a man who'd never experienced those qualities from his mother. But David had been *her* Musketeer, not Gusty's.

''She's a teacher.'' She put her feelings aside to reply honestly. ''Third grade. And she loves every one of those children and is always looking for ways to reach the difficult ones, to help the challenged ones, to make up for what the neglected ones miss at home.''

He liked what he was hearing; she could see it in his eyes .

''She's sort of a fifties housewife type,'' she went on. She may as well give him the whole truth. ''She bakes and gardens and loves being home. And you can drop in on her any time of the day or night, and her place is tidy.'' She smiled in self-deprecation. ''I hate that about her. I work at it, but my apartment always looks like it's been rifled by vandals.''

''I understand that. If I didn't have a housekeeper,

I'd be buried under magazines, newspapers and research materials.''

They finished lunch in silence. He stared out the window at the passersby, while she did her best not to think. The situation was too complex, too fraught with imminent disaster, to analyze and still remain sane.

She said a little prayer that Gusty was safe and would remain so until they found her, and that Aunt Sadie's death had just been an unfortunate accident. But there were still too many unanswered questions to allow for the comfort she was beginning to feel in David Hartford's company. He seemed as worried about Gusty as she was.

They drove through Arch Cape, Manzanita, Rockaway, Tillamook, and several little places in between, going up and down main streets and a few side streets, looking into restaurants, coffee shops, bakeries—with no sign of Gusty.

They continued to comb town after town until dark, then David headed for home.

''If she got this far,'' he said, watching the winding road in the darkness, ''we'll miss her anyway. We'll just use my house as a homebase and start again in the morning.''

''Okay.'' Athena lay her head wearily against the headrest, the sleepless night catching up with her. Exhaustion overtook worry and she fell asleep as the shadowy landscape sped past the windows.

DAVID PARKED THE CAR in the garage, walked around her side to open the door and gave her a gentle shake.

"Are you awake?" he asked.

She opened her eyes, looked straight at him and said very clearly, "Yes, I am." Then closed her eyes again and went right back to sleep.

He tried again. "Athena."

"Yeah?"

"We're home."

"Yeah."

"Can you walk into the house?"

"Yeah."

"Okay, let's…"

The sound of her quiet, sleepy breathing interrupted him.

All right. He accepted that he was going to have to handle this on his own.

He dug out his house key, put an arm between her back and the seat until he could turn her upper body sideways out of the car and lift her out without breaking her legs. Once he'd gotten her clear of the car, he steadied his grip on her, then walked toward the back door.

She wrapped both arms around his neck, her head resting comfortably on his shoulder.

"You awake?" he asked again.

"Yeah," she replied, then breathed a gentle little snore into his ear.

"Now, had I been with you the night of the party," he said to her as he struggled to hold her and turn the key in the narrow back door to the kitchen, "there probably wouldn't be a baby because you'd have been out cold then, too."

He flipped on the light, carried her across the

kitchen and up the back stairs. He sidled through the open door of the bedroom he'd promised he'd give her at the opposite end of the hallway from his and placed her in the middle of the bed.

In the light from the hallway, he pulled off her shoes, then covered her with an extra blanket from the closet shelf.

Her hair was everywhere—trapped under her, over the pillow, across her face and in her mouth. He worked gently to extricate it from between her lips, then brushed it from her face and eased her body forward against his shoulder to get the stream of hair out from under her and lay it over the pillow.

The scent of roses drifted around him, startling him.

He'd had this very dream, he thought a little weakly as he placed her back against the pillows, letting her hair fan out above her. Not with Athena, of course, but with Augusta, her hair all over him as they made love in his bed.

As though she'd tapped into his thoughts, Athena opened her eyes.

He straightened away from her, waiting for her shocked surprise, possibly even a criticism of his proximity, expecting to have to defend himself.

She looked around the room, then those remarkable blue eyes he remembered in Augusta rested on him. "Thank you," she said a little thickly. "I sleep like a rock."

"I noticed," he said. "Comfortable?"

"Yes."

"All right. I'm at the far end of the hall."

She smiled. "You keep your promises."

"Every one. Can you stay awake one more minute?"

She frowned at him sleepily. "Why?"

"Just lie still." He went to his room for his digital camera. She sat up suspiciously when he walked in with it. "Don't be alarmed. I've got a friend who might be able to help us find Gusty, but he can't do it without a photograph. And since you're identical…"

"Oh." She relaxed. He snapped the shot, then lowered the camera. "Perfect."

"But tell him she's softer looking than I am. That she wears long skirts and dresses and is always smiling." She stopped and sighed. "Of course, she might not be now."

"Try not to worry." He put the camera on the dresser and moved to the head of the bed to pull the blankets back up over her. "We're covering all the bases. Get some rest. We'll go out again in the morning."

"Okay." She gave him a thin smile. "Thanks. Good night, David." She turned onto her side, snuggled into the pillows and was asleep as quickly as she'd awakened.

He carried her bag into her room, put her shoes in the closet, then pulled the door partially closed.

He went to his office and called Henry Wren, an agent he'd worked with in Iraq early in his career. Henry had retired from the agency and now made a good living in private undercover work. With years of experience behind him and a network of contacts who owed him, he could locate anyone or anything.

Henry answered the phone with, "Davey? Is that really you?"

David smiled into the phone, not surprised that Henry knew it was him even though he'd had caller ID blocked on this number.

"Hey, Henry. How are you?"

"Old, rickety, celibate. Couldn't be much worse."

David laughed. "You're only fifty-five."

"Yeah, well. You know what they say. It's the mileage. Hang by your feet in an Iraqi prison for a week and see how old *you* feel."

"It was only two hours," David corrected, "and we got you out. Are you ever going to stop whining about that?"

"Guess I'll have to if it's not going to get me any more sympathy than you're showing. What do you want anyway?"

"A favor."

"After calling me a whiner?"

"Who cut you down in that Iraqi prison?"

Henry sighed dramatically. "Are you ever going to stop capitalizing on that? Okay, what do you need?"

"I need you to find someone." David explained about Gusty, the accident and her escape from the hospital with amnesia. "I'm faxing you her photograph and other details that might help you."

"This must be personal," Henry said, "since you're not in the business anymore."

"It is. I forgot to mention that she's seven months' pregnant."

"Ah. And why aren't you doing this yourself? You're a pretty good tracker, as I recall."

"Her twin sister is staying with me until she's found," he replied, "and I don't have quite the freedom to move that this kind of thing requires. We'll keep doing a regional search, but I saw no sign of her. Without her knowing who she is or where she belongs, she could wander anywhere. Will you do it?"

"Sure. But you know how iffy this kind of thing is when the trail's cold."

"Yeah. Just do your best, okay?"

"Okay."

David faxed Henry the photo and the details he'd promised, then went to bed.

He lay awake for hours with the knowledge that somewhere in the night, his baby was curled up in the womb of a woman who didn't know who she was or where to go.

The two people in the world who'd suddenly become the most precious people in his life were lost to him and he hated it. He didn't control much in this world, but he'd always promised himself that when he had a family, they would be secure in the knowledge that he loved and cared for them.

Had Augusta been coming to find him? he wondered. Was that how she'd ended up in the river? But if she'd been driving up from California, Astoria was one hundred and fifty miles north of Dancer's Beach.

Why hadn't she called or come sooner to tell him about the baby?

Why hadn't she told her sister?

Would she want to marry him? According to Athena's description, she was the kind of woman who would like being married, enjoy raising children and keeping a home—all the things a man dreamed of in his shamelessly chauvinistic fantasies.

Then a worrisome thought occurred to him. If she'd waited so long to tell him, maybe she *hadn't* found him as fascinating as he'd found her. Considering he'd passed out on her, he thought, that shouldn't be a surprise.

Maybe she was coming to tell him about the baby face-to-face, but didn't want him in her life.

Then what would he do? He didn't like the idea of having fathered a child he'd never see, whose development he couldn't influence and take part in.

He tried to quiet his thoughts and go to sleep. But the house had a different mood tonight. He was being foolish, he was sure, but he swore he could feel the difference.

There was a woman in the house. He remembered carrying Athena's soft, warm body from the car to the house, covering her with a blanket, trying to prevent her from hurting herself with that magnificent hair.

His mind was doing some kind of weird transference thing with her, he realized with concern. Probably because he couldn't find Augusta, the appearance of her identical sister was confusing his feelings.

He had to watch that, he thought guiltily. Or he'd alienate both women before he even knew if he had a chance with Augusta and his baby.

He lay on his back and tried not to think about

anything but getting to sleep. He rested an arm across his forehead and caught a whiff of spicy roses from his fingertips.

He frowned as sleep finally claimed him.

Chapter Five

Athena awoke to bars of sunshine coming through the venetian blinds. And not a sound coming from the house. From beyond it, she could hear the crash of the surf, but nothing else.

She looked around her at the room she used to occupy as a child. The dainty canopied bed had been replaced by a double sleigh bed. The lady's slipper chair covered in the same fabric as her pink bedspread was gone and in its place stood a big overstuffed blue-and-gold paisley chair.

On a small nightstand beside her bed stood the Mickey Mouse clock that used to wake her as a child. She was shocked to see that it read 11:15.

A dark wood four-drawer dresser held a French bouquet of silk flowers in a light blue pottery vase, and an old-fashioned ivory-and-gold comb-and-brush set complete with file, manicure scissors and button-hook.

Athena's bag had been placed on the floor near the small closet, and her jacket had been hung up inside. Her shoes stood neatly on the closet floor.

David Hartford was tidier than he claimed.

She walked down the corridor in her stockinged feet, momentarily distracted by the blank spot on the wall where the Degas that Sadie left Alexis had hung.

She went on to the office to which David had led her the night of the party, expecting to find him at work there. But it was empty.

David was not in the kitchen, either.

She could smell fresh coffee, though, and found a note propped up against the pot. It read in a printed-writing sort of style,

Athena,

Gone to check out where we left off last night and work my way home. You were sleeping so soundly, I didn't want to wake you. Please help yourself to anything in the fridge. I should be home by midafternoon.

I called all transportation in and out of Astoria and left Augusta's description. If anyone calls, please take a message—use the yellow pad by the phone.

Make yourself at home.

David

P.S. I know I promised you a vehicle, but if you want to go anywhere, it'd be safer to wait until I get home. The truck belongs to Trevyn, who is a little careless about maintenance, and the Jeep is Bram's. He has it "tweaked" for high performance. I'd like to have the truck looked over before you take it anywhere. D.

Presuming, she thought with just a shade of annoyance, that she wouldn't be able to handle the "tweaked" Jeep.

Athena opened cupboards until she found a plain, dark blue mug. She pulled it down by the handle and discovered that on the other side of it was a star pattern in gold and the words World's Greatest Lover printed on it.

Mmm. Was he in the habit of midnight trysts? She tried to imagine what the woman looked like who'd given it to him. A slender brunette, probably. Or a cool blonde.

Before she could get into serious speculation about that, she decided it was none of her business. She poured coffee into it and went through the mudroom in the back and down a narrow flight of stairs to the basement.

Since David was absent, she was going to check the smugglers' stairs, confident she'd find evidence of use. The door to the stairs that led down to the beach was in the west corner of the basement.

She walked around an island of neatly stacked packing boxes to the corner of the musty basement—and stared at the fresh brick in complete surprise.

There was no door.

Access to the smugglers' stairs had been sealed. Curious. She couldn't decide if that meant they weren't used anymore—even for frolics on the beach—or that they'd been sealed up to prevent interference from inside the house.

She stared at it in perplexity another moment, then went back upstairs to take a shower and form her next plan of attack.

Frankly, she didn't "feel" David Hartford was a criminal. And therefore that made it difficult to imagine that his friends would be. But she'd been trained to make determinations based on facts, not on feelings. And though she didn't have enough of those to know what to think about David, she had sufficient suspicions to keep her feelings in check.

She tried to call Lex, but all she got was her answering machine, the same message that she was out of town for several days spoken in impressively lovely Italian, then repeated in English.

Athena asked her to get in touch as soon as she was able. And on the chance that she'd lost or misplaced Athena's cell phone number—a distinct possibility with her artistic sister—she left that, too.

Then she called Patrick Connelly and told him what had happened to Gusty.

"The police are searching, and David Hartford has a friend looking also, but would you see what you can do?"

"Sure," he replied, though his tone wasn't encouraging. "Wandering somewhere on the Oregon coast without knowing who she is or where she's going."

Distilled down to the bare facts, the situation was grim.

"Yeah," she said.

"Okay, I'm on it."

Needing to occupy her mind, she decided to take one of the vehicles to look around Dancer's Beach on the chance Gusty had found her way here.

Showered and dressed, she noticed a hook on the

kitchen wall with keys and a St. Christopher medal hanging from it. She snatched the one labeled Jeep off the hook and ran down to the garages.

SHE DISCOVERED on the first turn that the Jeep had a very light touch and a lot of power. She might have lost control if she hadn't been prepared for it. She gave her complete attention to a long series of hairpin turns, then breathed a sigh of relief when she hit a straight stretch that led all the way to town.

Taking care to treat the vehicle with respect, she drove up and down the small business area's streets, watching for red hair and Gusty's very feminine walk. Where Lex moved like a dancer, Gusty had a natural sway to her hips that always attracted male attention. Athena and Lex used to tease her about it when they were teenagers, threatening to send her ahead of them to draw boys.

She walked through the ice cream parlor Gusty had once loved, the drugstore that still had a food counter, the coffee bar on the ground floor of the Buckley Arms apartment house.

No Gusty.

She walked through the antiques and collectables shop next door to the hotel because Gusty loved primitive kitchen tools, and had an old ladder hanging from the ceiling in her kitchen on which were suspended a large collection of graters, strainers, dippers and biscuit cutters.

The shop was empty except for an older couple studying the ugliest lamp Athena had ever seen.

As a gesture of confidence in her and David's ability to find Gusty, she walked down an aisle crowded with military memorabilia, looking for kitchen primitives.

She found them at the far end and searched the displays for the spoon egg whip with a wooden handle that Gusty had been searching for the past year. When they'd sent each other want lists last year before Christmas, Gusty had included an illustration cut out of an old Ward's catalogue. From what Athena could tell, it looked just like a spoon, except that it wouldn't hold anything. The spoon shape was formed of five or six thin wires with spaces between.

She was completely confounded when she found one—or thought she did. She picked it up and stared at it, certain this couldn't be it. She'd searched the East Coast and Gusty the West while Lex prowled the antique shops of Rome.

She noticed through the holes in the spoon that the woman who'd been looking at the lamp was now smiling at *her.*

There was a motherliness about her that Athena saw and felt.

Athena held up the tool. "Is this a spoon egg whip?" she asked.

The woman nodded. "Certainly is. I'm not into kitchen collectables myself, but my friend is and she has one."

"Oh, good." Athena found herself hugging the tool to her, absurdly happy that she'd found this little thing that somehow connected her to Gusty.

When she noticed that the woman was watching her face, almost as though she saw into her head, she explained with an embarrassed smile, "My sister's been looking all over for one of these."

"Well, wasn't that lucky?" She came around the end of the display table to offer her hand. "I'm Peg McKeon. That's my husband, Charlie." She pointed to the man holding the ugly lamp in one hand while looking through a shelf of books with the other. He came to be introduced.

"I'm Athena Ames," she said. "I'm just visiting for a few days."

"Us, too," Peg said. "Our kids have a summer place here, but they've all gone home now. So we have the place for a while." Peg put a hand to Athena's forehead. "You look worried."

Athena opened her mouth, the whole story on the tip of her tongue. Peg and Charlie looked as though they would hang on every word and possibly even solve her problems for her.

But it was simply parent envy, she realized just in time. Cuddly older women and calm, smiling older men always made her want to spill her guts like the child who had to tell someone about the terrors inside.

She smiled. "I'm fine, thank you. I was up all night last night traveling, and I'm pooped. It was nice to meet you, though. You're buying the lamp?"

It was about two and a half feet high, the base formed in the shape of a cupid that held a plump oil fount worked in a fussy design. The whole was topped by a wide red silky lamp shade with an eight-inch chiffon border embroidered with colorful little flowers.

It was truly hideous.

Charlie held it up proudly. "Quite a find, eh? We'll just leave it in the house as a surprise for the kids."

"We always try to find them something special," Peg said with a very sincere conviction that it was, "because they're all so special to us. We have three sons who've married the most wonderful girls and presented us with a growing raft of grandchildren."

"And we have one daughter," Charlie added with a rueful smile, "who can't seem to get the message. Even her boyfriend's given up on her."

Athena felt a little sympathy for the daughter, but offered it instead to them, knowing that they simply wanted her to be as happy as their sons were.

"She'll find someone," Athena said. "Everyone does."

"Have you?" Peg asked abruptly.

She smiled and backed toward the counter. "Everyone except me. It was nice to meet you."

"You, too, dear. Come and see us. We're in the old Buckley house. Anyone can tell you where it is."

"Thank you," she replied. "But I probably won't be here long enough."

Athena paid for her purchase, then waved at the McKeons as she left the shop.

She mused that grown children who'd had poor parents should be allowed to share the parents of their contemporaries who'd been blessed with good ones but could just spend part of their time with them. It seemed only fair that the parentally challenged be allowed access to them the rest of the time.

LOST IN THOUGHTS of her sisters on her way home, Athena didn't notice the curve until she was on it.

Fortunately there was no traffic as she took the curve too widely, hit the soft roadside covered in pine needles and dropped the Jeep onto its side like a roped calf.

She screamed and hung sideways, suspended from her seat belt. For an instant she couldn't breathe, and could hear herself saying, "Oh, no! Oh, no! Oh, no!"

Then realizing, after a moment, that she was fine, she told herself firmly to shut up, unbuckled her belt and pulled herself easily to her feet on the roadside. She flexed her arms and legs while her heartbeat slowed its hammering. She didn't even seem to be bruised.

She checked her purse for her cell phone and mercifully found it intact. Then she realized she had no idea who to call. She had the D.C. emergency numbers in her purse but that wouldn't help here.

She should call David, but she hadn't noted his number.

Reluctantly, she dialed 9-1-1.

DAVID SUSPECTED TROUBLE the moment the garage door opened and he saw that the Jeep was gone. He didn't think it meant Bram was back. When David had tried to reach Bram again this morning on his cell phone, the readout said there were no receivers in his location.

He'd picked up steaks for dinner on the way home and put those in the refrigerator, then looked around the house, just in case.

But Athena wasn't there. And she hadn't left a note.

He battled against instinctive annoyance. He'd warned her about the truck and the Jeep.

That didn't mean she had to listen, he reminded himself. She was an adult, an attorney with her own firm. And she was worried about her sister. She'd probably set off to search on her own since he'd left without her this morning.

He looked at the clock. Five-eighteen.

It was almost six when the telephone rang.

"Mr. Hartford, this is the 9-1-1 dispatcher."

His heart sank to his stomach.

"Your houseguest is fine," she said in a quiet, calming voice, "but she's had an accident."

"Where is she?" he demanded.

"Still with the car, I believe. The tow truck's just arriving. Her vehicle is on its side at the hairpin turns between your location and Dancer's Beach."

"I'm on my way," he said, and hung up the phone.

He wasn't sure why anger was taking the place of reason as he ran to his car and raced off in her direction. She wasn't his business, Gusty was.

Maybe it was because he couldn't find Gusty, but Athena was handy.

By the time he reached the accident site, the Jeep was already attached to the tow truck, and several police officers talked with the operator while Athena stood by in a silky white blouse and the blue knit pants, arms folded, looking depressed and demoralized.

His anger was defused by half.

He turned around and pulled up behind her.

She watched his approach with a defensive tilt of

her chin. He enjoyed the confusion in her eyes when he asked her simply if she was all right. She studied him suspiciously while rubbing her arms against the early evening breeze

"I'm fine," she finally replied. She pointed reluctantly toward the Jeep, now hiked up behind the truck. "I'll pay for the damages. Externally, at least, it doesn't look too bad."

"Dave!" the tow truck driver shouted at him, leaning out of the driver's side window.

David pointed Athena to his car. "Get in," he said. "I'll be back in a minute."

Rusty Browning had towed Trevyn's truck when they'd first arrived in Dancer's Beach. He'd bought it for cheap transportation, but it had major problems. It had died on Trevyn on a trip south to photograph rock formations off the coast.

Rusty had towed him in, David and Bram had driven to Rusty's office to pick up Trevyn, they'd all started talking about trucks and fishing, and the four had played pool together once a week since then.

"Doesn't look too bad," Rusty said. He was a huge man with red hair who did his work with the skill and care one might expect to find in a goldsmith. "You want me to take it to Beach Mechanics?"

"Yeah, thanks."

Rusty angled his chin in Athena's direction. "Bram's girl?"

David shook his head. "No. I just told her she could use the Jeep while he's gone."

"Ah." Rusty grinned. "Your girl."

"No."

Rusty looked puzzled for a minute, then apparently decided it didn't matter. "Whoever's girl she is," he said with a wink, "she needs to be more careful." Then he winked. "Probably no use telling her, though. Redheads, you know." He pointed to his own coppery sideburns, all that was visible under his baseball cap. "Liable to take your head off."

David laughed his understanding. "Thanks, Rusty."

He turned to one of the police officers preparing to climb back into his vehicle.

"She's free to go?" he asked.

The officer nodded. "She refused a ride to the emergency room. She says she isn't even bruised. Your car?"

"Belongs to a friend of mine who left it in my care," David replied. "I told her she could use it."

The officer nodded. "Okay. Good night, Mr. Hartford."

"Good night, Officer."

David headed back to his car as the officer drove away.

"I'm sorry," Athena said again as he slipped in behind the wheel. "I was kind of getting the hang of it, but I was thinking about Gusty and everything..."

"You read the note," he said quietly, putting the key in the ignition. "I asked you to wait."

"My sister's missing!" she said, temper snapping. "I didn't want to wait!"

He guessed it had been a long couple of hours for her. But he felt as though it had been an eternity since he'd seen a very pregnant Gusty on television yesterday morning, and understanding what drove Athena and reacting to it properly were two entirely different things.

"Consequently you've risked your life," he replied quietly, with a stiff element of censure in his tone, "damaged somebody else's car, and inconvenienced a lot of people."

"You mean *you!*" she shouted. "Because the policemen and the truck driver were very courteous and just doing their jobs. Well, I'm sorry you had to trouble yourself to come and get me. You invited me here, but obviously this isn't going to work since you took off without me this morning and resent having to drive a couple of miles to pick me up!" She pushed open the car door. "I'll let you know where to send my—"

She tried to get out of the car, but he caught her arm and pulled her back inside, thinking he should have taken Rusty's warning more seriously.

As he'd suspected on the drive over here, she was upset that he'd gone off without her.

"I let you sleep in," he said reasonably, "because I thought you needed the rest. This could be a long haul."

She put a hand to her mouth and closed her eyes. He got the feeling if her hand hadn't been there, she'd be sobbing.

In a moment she was composed again. "I'm sorry about the car," she repeated.

"It's all right," he said, eager to make amends. Acting judgmental in order to give his own frustration an outlet had been a cheap shot. "Damage looks minimal. You sure you don't have to see a doctor?"

"I'm sure."

He turned out onto the road in the direction of home. "Where'd you go?"

"I thought she might have come to Dancer's Beach." Her window was slightly open and she closed it, rubbing at her arms again. "So I just looked around."

Checking his rearview mirror, he slowed to a crawl, pulled off his sweatshirt and handed it to her.

"Thanks, but I don't..." she began to protest.

"Put it on," he insisted. "Warm up your muscles. You think you're fine, but that jolt's going to hurt in the morning."

He kept the slow pace while she unfastened her seat belt, pulled the sweatshirt on and buckled herself in again. Then he picked up speed.

She rubbed her arms and leaned her head against the rest. She gave him a tired smile. "Thank you. That is better."

He looked at her chunky heeled leather pumps and her elegant slacks. "I think you have to be outfitted for detective work," he said. "Tomorrow we'll head south, and pick up some things for you on the way."

"This is comfortable," she disputed.

He eyed her skeptically. "Don't you own jeans and tennis shoes?"

"No. I have no place to wear them. I have to look professional for work. Most of my spare time not spent in overtime is spent socializing with these same people who just don't picnic or frolic at the beach.

It's Washington, D.C. The atmosphere is urgent and...I don't know...dressy.''

"Then you've never been truly comfortable. Trust me. Jeans will relax you.''

"I don't believe clothes can relax you.''

"Why not? If suits can make you feel ready for the courtroom, why can't the right clothes make you feel ready to relax?''

She closed her eyes. This man, she decided, posed too many questions.

HE GRILLED STEAKS and made a salad for dinner while she set the small, round table in a corner of the kitchen. She found A.1. sauce and Worcestershire in the refrigerator door and put those in the middle of the table.

"Salad dressing?" she asked.

"Top shelf," he said, putting the steaks onto plates. "Way in the back.''

He put the steaks on the table, then brought their salad bowls and a pair of empty cups.

Athena went for the fresh coffee she'd made while he was cooking.

She ate hungrily. She'd had a biscotti with her coffee while she'd been driving around Dancer's Beach, then forgot to have lunch when she discovered the antiques shop.

She told him about Peg and Charlie McKeon. "They were buying the ugliest lamp and seemed so proud of it. They're going to leave it as a gift for their kids at the summer house they let them use. But they were so sweet. They thought the lamp was special and they were giving it to their kids because they thought *they* were special, too.'' She sighed. ''I wonder what it's like to have parents like that.''

''I don't know.'' David stacked up pieces of lettuce on his fork. ''But my baby will.''

For the first time since this whole complex intrigue had begun, Athena realized that he was going to be crushed when he found out the baby wasn't his.

''You're that sure the baby is yours,'' she asked, wanting to guage his reaction.

''I am,'' he replied confidently. ''The doctor said twenty-nine weeks. I counted back. It's me.''

''But you...you were with Gusty only once. She could have gone back to Pansy Junction and been with someone else.''

''Pansy Junction,'' he repeated with a grin. ''I heard you tell Holden that was where she lives. Sounds like a name out of a children's book.''

She had to smile, too. ''Really. There have been pansies in the town square since the town was founded during the Gold Rush.''

''You said you weren't aware that Augusta had a boyfriend,'' he reminded her.

She nodded. ''But I also wasn't aware she was pregnant. Anyway, Gusty might have different ideas about raising her baby. I mean, if she didn't even tell you, tell the baby's father she was pregnant...''

''Doesn't matter. Now I know. I'm going to be in the picture, one way or another.''

She sat quietly, thinking that did not bode well for the day he learned the truth.

They finished dinner in silence. Athena wrestled

quietly with guilt while she cleared the table, then wiped it off.

David put their few dishes in the dishwasher.

"There were no messages when you came home?" Athena asked. "From Holden or anybody?"

He shook his head as he dried his hands on a towel. "Nothing."

Athena had a sudden thought.

"You know," she said, pushing the chairs in against the table. "Gusty used to love the outlet mall in Lincoln City."

"She did?"

He looked surprised, then she realized he'd be wondering why she loved to go there when she'd lived in Northern California. He didn't know about their childhood summers at Cliffside.

"Yeah," she said. "When she visited the friends she had here, they always took a day to go to Lincoln City."

He seemed to accept that, but asked with a puzzled frown, "But why would she wake up, realize that she didn't know who she was or where she belonged—and decide to go *shopping?*"

"Maybe she just remembered the place," she said hopefully. Then she smiled, trying not to sound as desperate as she felt. "Maybe a woman's shopping instinct survives even amnesia." She sobered just as suddenly. "Or is that too absurd?"

He patted her shoulder consolingly. "I don't know. But it's something. We'll go first thing in the morning and we'll scour every shop."

She leaned against the edge of the counter and

stared into her coffee. ''You know what I worry about?'' she said, almost to herself.

''What?'' he asked. He leaned toward her, worry about Gusty something they shared.

''What she does at night.'' She looked out at the darkness and felt an ache in the pit of her stomach. ''She doesn't know anybody. She doesn't have any money.''

''I know.'' He put a hand to her back between her shoulder blades and rubbed gently. ''But don't do that. It'll make you crazy. There are shelters everywhere along the coast. Hopefully she's found one, or someone's directed her there.''

''Yeah. Hopefully.''

He pointed her toward the back stairs. ''Why don't you take a hot bath to ward off muscle stiffness, then go to bed early?''

''But there's no tub in my bathroom.''

''There is in mine. You're welcome to use it. I'll be down here for a couple of hours. I'm going to do some editing, just to give myself something else to think about.''

''You're sure?''

''Yes. Go ahead.''

DAVID TRIED TO WORK, but despite his assurances to Athena, he kept thinking about Gusty, cold and alone, and prayed she'd find Good Samaritans along her way. He gave up the effort after about an hour and went upstairs, noticing as he passed Athena's room that her door was open and her bed still unoccupied.

He went into his office, half-expecting to hear her

puttering in the bathroom, but there wasn't a sound coming from that direction.

The door was partially open and the bathroom light brightened that corner of the room.

"Athena?" he called.

No answer.

He went closer to the door. "Athena?" he said again, a little louder.

Nothing.

He peered around the corner and saw the back of her head, her yard of hair wrapped into a loose knot on top, leaning against the rim of the old ball-and-claw-foot tub.

He tiptoed in and saw that she was fast asleep.

Trying to ignore the slender, supple body under the thin remnant of suds, he dipped his fingertips into the water and found that it was cold.

He looked to the hook on the back of the door and saw that she'd brought the short robe he'd left her last night. But he decided this required his double-thick, full-length robe.

He went to his closet and brought it back, then knelt beside the tub and put his thumb and forefinger to her chin. It took superhuman effort to ignore the small breasts blooming out of the water.

"Athena!" he said loudly.

Her eyes flew open. "What?" she demanded, sitting up.

"You fell asleep and the water's cold," he said, taking her arm in his hand and helping her stand. He wrapped the robe around her like a towel and she leaned into him, asleep again.

He swung her up into his arms, half amused, half worried. She must live her life in a constant state of exhaustion. Either that, or she was narcoleptic. He'd never met anyone who could be awake one instant and asleep the next like she could.

He carried her to her bed, thinking that she'd been here a little more than twenty-four hours and it was already becoming a habit.

He rubbed the fabric gently, impersonally, over her arms and down her legs, then opened out the blanket she'd folded neatly at the foot of the bed, spread it over her, and tugged the wet robe out from under her. She rolled over in the process, still asleep.

He pulled the pins out of her hair and let it fall down her back.

Then, because that was all the torture and confusion he could stand for one evening, he grabbed the wet robe in one fist, walked out of the room and closed the door.

Chapter Six

Athena awoke to the tantalizing aromas of bacon frying and coffee brewing and leaped right out of bed.

She stopped halfway to the bathroom, looking down at her naked body. How had that happened?

She remembered being in the bathtub, then...nothing. Oh, Lord. David had pulled her out of the bathtub and put her to bed.

Falling asleep on him the day before when she'd been fully clothed had been one thing. But this was really embarrassing.

She showered quickly, aware of a little muscle soreness where the shoulder harness had held her in place during the accident. Apart from that, she felt fine—and lucky.

She jumped into gray pin-striped slacks and a pink sweater with a cowl neck. The pants had a matching jacket, but that wouldn't fit the relaxed image David was encouraging.

She brushed her hair and caught it at the nape of her neck with a handcrafted silver clasp that had been a gift from Lex.

Oregon was doing this to her, she thought as she

hurried down the stairs. At home she was in complete control at all times—in or out of the courtroom. And while she sometimes grew tired of the need to be that way, it was who she was and she'd accepted it.

She didn't like wrecking someone else's car, falling asleep at the drop of a hat, or looking silly.

She decided to confront the issue head-on and get it out of the way.

"Good morning," she said briskly to David as she walked into the kitchen. He stood at the stove, breaking eggs into a cast-iron frying pan. "I apologize for falling asleep on you."

He turned away from the stove, an egg poised over the edge of the pan. His dark eyes were amused though he was careful not to smile.

Okay. He was right. That had sounded...suggestive. "I meant..." she began.

He cut her off. "No need to explain or apologize. Eggs up or over?"

"Over hard, please." Fine. She wouldn't apologize. She glanced at the table to see if there was anything still to be done. No silverware. She went to the drawer and took knives and forks to the table.

"I've never seen anyone sleep as deeply as you do," he said.

It had been a joke among her sisters since they were children. "Just tell me I don't snore." She went for cups and poured coffee.

He turned over the eggs and while they cooked, he carried cream and sugar to the table.

"Well, not loudly anyway," he said with a smile

at her before he turned back to the stove. "You sleep as though you have a clear conscience."

She ignored that remark. She was too guilty on all fronts in this situation to pretend otherwise. But she had to be watchful until she knew what was going on here.

He took a plate out of the oven, served her eggs onto it and placed it in front of her. "Careful," he said. "Plate's hot."

Then he added as he carried his own plate to the table, "You're not blaming yourself again for Gusty's absence, are you?"

Yes, she was. And it would be such a comfort to admit that. But then she'd have to let go of her suspicions, admit other things she wasn't yet comfortable saying, so she simply shrugged. "I've always felt responsible for them."

She hadn't even noticed what she'd said until he looked up from peppering his eggs. "Them? I thought there were only two of you."

Be careful! she chided herself.

"I meant, my sister and my father." She acted casually, spreading blackberry jam on whole wheat toast. "He was a gentle soul and needed protection against the world." That was true and came off sounding very genuine.

Mercifully, David bought it. They traded the pepper and the jam.

"Nobody can be responsible for the whole world." He snapped off half a bacon strip and chewed and swallowed. "That's self-destructive. I used to feel that way, but you have to learn to accept your limits or you'll go insane." Her eggs were perfect. She took several bites, then sipped her coffee and asked, "Is that why you quit being a reporter?"

He hesitated, as though carefully considering his answer. "Yes. Someone…important to Trevyn and me died because we were betrayed by someone else we trusted. I should have seen it coming."

"Who can foresee betrayal?" she asked. "That's something you can't protect yourself against because it's entirely someone else's responsibility."

"In life, maybe," he said, "but in…in that line of work you try to foresee everything or—well, it's dangerous."

"I didn't realize being a reporter was so dangerous that people around you die," she said challengingly.

He held her gaze. "Neither did I."

"I'm sorry." She was exasperated with his unwillingness to tell her more, but found herself wanting to share what worried him. And there was something painful in his eyes when he talked about it. "Was it someone you loved?"

"We all loved her," he said, staring into his cup. "She was beautiful and brave and funny. But she was Trevyn's girl."

"Does he blame you?"

He shook his head. "I blame me. I was in charge."

"Ah, so you don't practice what you preach?"

"Pardon me?"

"You can't be responsible for the whole world," she repeated his words to him. "It's self-destructive. You have to learn your limitations or you'll go insane. That doesn't apply to you?"

He opened his mouth to reply, then quirked an eyebrow, suppressed a grin and pointed with his fork at her plate. "Eat your breakfast," he said.

All right. Score one for her.

THEY WERE IN LINCOLN CITY by midmorning and methodically worked their way from one end of the outlet mall to the other, shop by shop, on the premise that if Gusty had come here, she might have tried to get a job. With her wallet at the bottom of the river, she would need employment.

By late afternoon there'd still been no sign of her.

David felt bitter disappointment, but Athena looked so grim, he didn't want to burden her with his despair.

And he had to remember to be careful when he talked to her about his work. He had to remember which part of it she knew.

"Come on," he said, taking her arm. "We'll buy you those jeans and tennis shoes we talked about yesterday, so that tomorrow we can check out Lincoln City proper."

Her consent was halfhearted.

He took her back to Your Neck of the Woods, a large, warehouse like store that had everything for the serious outdoorsman—or woman.

David was happy to wander through the camping gear while she tried on the many cuts and styles of jeans. It was a time-consuming task.

He came back once to check on her and found her staring into a three-way mirror while wearing pencil-slim jeans that hugged her hips and thighs flatteringly. Her hair had obviously become a problem during the trying-on process because she'd pinned it up at the back of her head.

"That cowl neck's too dressy," the clerk said. "Try this gray rib-knit henley. With your hair it'll look wonderful."

She'd given David a doubtful look. "The jeans are too tight, aren't they?"

"No, they're not," he assured her. That was not the question to ask a fanny-man. He wandered back into the camping gear.

When he returned half an hour later, she had her back to the mirror while the clerk zipped and buttoned her into a long cotton dress with a dark blue background sprigged with little flowers. It hugged her bosom and fell loosely to her ankles.

"This isn't me," she protested as the clerk struggled with a button. "I'm just not..."

"Well, wait until you see it," the clerk insisted, finally succeeding with the button and smoothing the shoulders. "You're going to love it. You're just not used to wearing soft clothes."

Athena spotted David on the sidelines and rolled her eyes at him. "Me, in soft clothes," she said.

She looked charming. "I like it," he told her.

"I'd be tripping all over myself." She raised her head as she prepared to turn toward the mirror, but something seemed to catch her attention across the store and she froze, a small gasp of surprise parting her lips.

"David!" she whispered, pointing across the store.

"What?" Everything tensed inside him as he followed her pointing finger. But all he could see were groups of people shopping, mannequin torsos on the tops of counters, signs guiding shoppers to various departments.

"Gusty!" she shouted, a light going on inside her as she tore away from the clerk and ran down the store's crowded middle aisle.

While everyone nearby stood openmouthed, he followed her at a run as she pushed big men aside, sidled through tight little knots of people, eased by children, then set off at a run again as the aisle opened up for a space.

Taller than she, he could see over the top of her head as she pushed her way through a group of teen-aged boys studying a camp stove. He scanned the far side of the room for some sign of the woman she'd spotted from across the store.

She continued to run, shouting, as though she still saw her. He stayed right behind her, though he saw no one.

And then he realized what she thought she'd seen.

They approached a wall of mirrors near the men's dressing rooms, and in it, he saw Athena running toward herself in the unfamiliar dress, the state of her nerves and her desperate need to see her sister apparently conjuring her up out of her own reflection.

She stopped abruptly several feet away, looking at herself in horror. Then disappointment that it wasn't Gusty after all superceded her embarrassment and her face crumpled.

He put an arm around her shoulders and bustled her past a pair of staring women and into an open dressing room. He yanked the curtain the length of

the rod to afford them privacy and took her into
his arms.

"IT WAS *ME!*" She wept into his shoulder, pounding her fist once into his free one. "I thought it was
her and it was only...me!"

He had no idea what to say to her, so he simply
held her while she came apart in his arms. She wept
for five minutes while holding onto fistfuls of the
back of his sweater as though certain he was going
to try to escape.

But he held his ground—and her—for the duration.

She'd become a total idiot, Athena thought while
hearing herself sobbing like one. She hadn't wept like
this when her parents died, though she'd felt great
grief over the loss of any opportunity to make her
relationship with them right.

Since then she'd lost cases, she'd lost boyfriends,
she'd missed her sisters, her aunt, the perfect man
she'd never found, the babies she'd never had—but
she'd never cried like this for them.

She had to be sublimating something into this, she
thought as she continued to weep. This couldn't be
all for Gusty because deep down, she knew she was
out there somewhere, waiting to be found.

It was while she tried to call a halt to this repre-
hensible behavior and it refused to comply that she
became aware of the arms around her and the comfort
they provided.

And as soon as she registered that sensation, her
sobs quieted.

She felt his cheek against the top of her head and

his hand moving gently up and down her spine as he told her over and over that it was all right, that they would find Gusty, that she just had to trust him.

It felt so good for once to have someone comfort her. She turned off all thought for several moments and simply enjoyed the fact that he felt so big that, for a few moments at least, she could hide in his embrace. The way his body cradled her weight, the way his hands moved gently over her.

But all that sweetness changed in an instant. Actually, she reconsidered, it didn't change, she just suddenly became aware of something else.

Aware of how warm and hard the muscles of his arms were, how strong the thighs were that practically supported her, and yet how tender his touch was— and she'd begun to speculate about how it would feel if he touched her with passion rather than tenderness.

She sighed against him at the thought, letting her mind travel along that path for a moment.

And that was apparently when he became aware that the tenor of their embrace had changed. The arms around her were suddenly filled with tension and he used them to push her a step away as he took a step back.

She wanted to explain, but how did she go about telling him the whole complicated story in the tiny dressing room of a store crowded with shoppers?

He handed her his handkerchief. "I'll take you out to the car," he said. "Then I'll go pay for your things."

He looked confused, angry.

She didn't know how to help him or herself. "I

think I left my purse on the counter,'' she said, ''with the things I was going to buy.''

''All right. Let's go.'' He took her firmly by the arm, led her to the doors with a shoulder between her and all interested onlookers, and walked her to the car. ''I'll be right back,'' he said, and locked her door.

David wasn't sure if he was locking her in or himself out. This wasn't good. It had to be the inherent confusion about twins, but it was getting stronger rather than evening out.

He wanted Athena even more than he'd wanted Gusty the night of the party.

Big mistake. Gusty was carrying his baby. And he'd promised Athena she could stay with him until they found Gusty. He didn't see how this situation could get worse.

Until they got home and he found his little brothers, two backpacks and a big black mutt, sitting on the front steps.

Chapter Seven

The dog stood in front of the boys and barked menacingly as David pulled up beside a Yellow cab.

Brandon, 12, caught the dog's collar and commanded him to sit. Brady, 10, launched himself at David as he climbed out of the car.

Brady had dark eyes and curly, dark hair and a smile that could light up the universe. He was the result of his mother's alliance with the captain of her yacht, which was moored in Mexico City.

"Hi, Dave!" he said, wrapping his arms around David's middle. "I'm glad you're home! We were beginning to think you'd gone away, or something."

The boy's grip did feel a little desperate. David knew from personal experience that having a wealthy mother did not guarantee a child a sense of security—particularly when that child didn't see her for days.

"It's good to see you guys," he said, holding Brady to him, "but I thought you weren't coming back until Christmas."

Brandon appeared behind Brady, the dog following. "We had to come now," he said simply, "before they sent us away."

Brandon had stick-straight platinum hair and light blue eyes, the son of a Scandinavian industrialist who'd paid handsomely to rid his life of the boy's mother. Arne Bjork had been husband number three.

Brandon was less effusive than Brady, more cautious. He tried to put a brave face on their mother's emotional neglect, but he wasn't fooling anyone. David had done the same thing for years and understood him completely.

"Sent you away?" David asked. "You mean, she married the boyfriend?" He knew Jordana Hartford Meyer Bjork Sullivan Venturini's current love was disliked by both boys, and their pervading fear this past year had been that she would marry him.

Brandon nodded. "Three weeks ago in Vegas. Now he thinks he can run our lives."

In ordinary circumstances, an advisor would tell the boys to give their new stepfather a chance. But considering the choices Jordana made, the boys were probably justified in being resentful. David had yet to meet husband number six.

Brandon scratched the big black dog between the ears. "He took Ferdie to the pound for getting mud in the kitchen."

For just an instant David saw the pain Brandon's separation from the dog had cost him.

"When did you get Ferdie?"

"He followed us home from the park about a month ago."

"Don't you think it's stupid to send him away," Brady asked, "when you can wash the floor? And

Darby's not even the one who has to do it. Or Mom, either.''

David reached down to let the dog sniff his hand. It looked like a Great Dane-Saint Bernard mix with a large black-and-white face and an all black body that was tall but lean. The combination made him look as though he'd been mistakenly assembled with parts that didn't fit.

"I found him at the park," Brandon said. "And Mom told me I could keep him."

"Yeah," Brady said, "but that was before she married Darby. Now he's changing everything."

Ferdie sniffed David's hand and began to wag his tail.

David stroked the dog's head and had his other hand bathed in return.

"Good boy, Ferdie," Brandon said. "He's a friend."

At that the dog stood, front paws on David's chest, and kissed his face. His tongue was the widest thing David had ever seen. His breath also had a certain "bigness" to it.

"Ah, 'scuse me," an older man's voice said. It was the cab driver. He looked at David with suspicion and mild hostility. "Kids, here, told me you'd stand good for the cab ride from the airport. If that ain't true..."

Brady smiled with all the charm he could muster, and Brandon met David's eyes apologetically.

"I will." David dug out his wallet. "How much?"

The cost of the ride from the Portland Airport to the coast was staggering.

"Wow!" Brady exclaimed.

David gave the cabbie another twenty. "Thanks for getting them here safely," he said. "I know it isn't every driver who'd have picked them up. And thanks for waiting with them."

The cabbie tipped a woolen houndstooth cap. "Got no kids of my own, but if I did, I wouldn't let 'em wander around the countryside."

David nodded. "You're absolutely right. Thanks again."

With a smile the man climbed back into his cab, made a big circle in the driveway and drove off.

David returned his attention to the boys. "Does your mother know where you are? When did you leave, anyway?"

"We left this morning while Mom was still sleeping," Brandon replied. "We took our bikes to the pound when it opened, got Ferdie, then left our bikes there and called a cab to take us to the airport. I used all the cash I'd stashed to run away buying the plane tickets and shipping Ferdie."

"How did you get tickets?" David asked.

Brandon shrugged. "Taylor Park's dad is a travel agent. Taylor knows how to use the computer. I'll pay you back for the cab."

"He can't use his trust fund until he's eighteen." Brady stated the legal stipulations on the millions of dollars Brandon's father had set up for him. "Otherwise, we'd have gone to France."

It wasn't an important question at the moment, but David couldn't help himself. "Why France?"

"The Tour de France," the boys said simultaneously. Their bikes were their lives.

"Can we stay here for a while?" Brady asked, suddenly serious. His eyes said a lot of things David understood instinctively. *We're lost. We're afraid. We have nowhere else to turn.*

Brandon shook his head impatiently at his younger brother. "I told you to let *me* ask him," he said.

Brady didn't see the problem. "Well, what's the difference who...?"

"Because you don't just ask," Brandon explained. "You have to offer something."

"Whoa." David put an arm around Brandon's shoulders. The sad message in Brady's eyes was echoed in his, only more so because he was more sensitive, a little more needful of attention and affection. "We're talking about me, remember? Not our mother."

Brandon nodded. "I know. But you were working on that book when we came for spring break. We'll be in the way, and Ferdie will get mud in the—" He stopped abruptly as he suddenly noticed Athena still standing on the far side of the car. He looked into David's eyes, his own panicky. "You've got a girlfriend," he said.

David gestured Athena to join them. "No, but this is a friend, Athena Ames. Athena—Brandon and Brady."

Athena smiled warmly at the boys.

Brady returned her smile and shook hands. Brandon studied her coolly, shook her hand then quickly withdrew his.

The dog came forward to lick her hand when she

reached down to scratch his ears. He whined and wagged his tail.

"Do you live here?" Brady asked.

"Only temporarily," she replied, straightening.

"I'm helping her find someone," David explained with a simplicity he hoped would stave off questions.

He should have known better.

"Who?" Brady wanted to know.

"Her sister," David said.

"Is that why you were at the airport?" Brandon asked.

David shook his head. "I wasn't at the airport."

"No." Brandon pointed to Athena. "I mean her. I saw her at the airport."

For an instant, David didn't know what to say. Then he remembered what a bright, perceptive kid Brandon was. He heard Athena's intake of breath. "You're sure? Because Athena's sister is a twin. She looks just like her."

"Yeah," Brandon agreed. "She sure does."

"You saw her just today? While you were at the airport in Portland?"

"Yeah," Brandon replied. "She was with this kind of scary-looking guy. I noticed them because she had this long denim coat just like Mom wears and I thought for a minute that me and Brady were busted."

David felt a chill run down his spine. "Scary looking?"

"Sort of. He was looking all around like he didn't want anyone to notice. That's why I thought he was with Mom. Till she turned around."

"Did she seem scared?"

"No."

"Oh, David!" Athena gasped.

David held a hand out to her but needed more answers.

"Where were you? Which terminal?"

"Northwest."

"Where was she when you saw her?"

"At the baggage claim thing." He made a turning sign with his index finger.

"The baggage carousel."

"Yeah. The next one over from us." He pointed to the bat sticking out of the pack David still held for him. "We were carrying our packs, but I had to check the bat. I guess they thought it could be a weapon, or something."

"Oh, God." Athena clutched David's arm. "It's her. She has that coat! David..."

David patted her hand. "Easy," he cautioned. "Everything she had with her was lost in the river. She wouldn't have the coat. Brandon, what time was this?"

"Our flight came in at 12:35 this afternoon."

"What did this scary-looking guy look like? Do you remember? Tall? Short? Dark?"

Brandon frowned, trying to think. "I didn't really pay much attention to him. He was tall, but not as tall as you. Lighter hair. His eyes were what was scary. Like he was mad. But that's all I remember."

"Oh, David." Athena was tugging on his arm.

"Okay. Easy." He put an arm around her because she looked as though she was about to levitate. "Why don't you go in and call Officer Holden and we'll be right behind you.''

"Where'd her sister go?'' Brady wanted to know.

"We don't know,'' David explained, shouldering their packs. "She was in an accident and she hit her head and lost her memory. Now she's missing.''

"You mean missing,'' Brady asked, eyes widening, "like kidnapped?''

"We're not sure.''

"Wow!''

Brandon elbowed him. "It's a scary thing, dufus, not exciting.''

Brady elbowed him back. "I just meant I never met anybody who had a missing sister before. And if you were missing I wouldn't look for you.''

"Oh, yeah? Well, I didn't have to bring you, but I did, didn't I?''

For one moment it was clear in Brady's eyes that there'd been a time when he thought he might be left behind. "Yeah. I can't help it if I don't have a trust fund. You just got lucky.''

Brandon made a scornful sound. "Yeah. Real lucky.'' Then he turned to David as they walked into the living room and Athena excused herself and went into the kitchen. David closed the door. Brandon glanced at Brady. "Can he go upstairs so you and I can discuss business?''

"Business?'' David asked.

"Yeah, sorta. Family business.''

David handed Brady his pack. "You want to go on ahead, sport, so we can talk?''

Brady rolled his eyes and reclaimed his pack. "Can I get an apple or something first? I'm starving."

At David's nod, he headed for the kitchen.

"I like it here best," Brandon observed as they watched Brady walk away. "Better than Chicago. I'm glad you weren't gone on a trip, or something."

"Yeah, me too," David answered.

Brandon was speaking quietly, as though he had something secretive to share, so David remained with him in the little alcove near the door and the privacy it provided. The dog settled down at Brandon's feet. "What's up?" David's brain was trying to work on the fact that his brother might have spotted Gusty, but he forced it down to focus on him.

Brandon nodded. "My interest." He took a book out of his jacket pocket and handed it to David.

"What's this?"

"It's my trust fund." He folded his arms. He looked tired and stressed, David thought. The trip had clearly been a lark for Brady, but for Brandon, who'd had to plan everything, and carry it all off in an adult world without adult assistance, it had apparently been difficult and probably scary. He looked David in the eye. "Nobody can touch it until I'm eighteen, like Brady says, but you can have it on my eighteenth birthday if we can stay here until then. I'll sign something if you want."

David wasn't entirely surprised by Brandon's "deal." Every time the boys visited him, they wheedled and cajoled to stay longer, and they'd started visiting at spring break and at Christmas, as well as a month during the summer.

But he was surprised by the tears that stood in Brandon's eyes.

"I heard them talking, and they want to send us to boarding school," Brandon went on. "Me to an expensive one someplace in New York, and Brady to one in the Midwest that doesn't cost as much 'cause he doesn't have the trust fund." On the chance that David didn't understand what that meant to him, he added anxiously, "Not only are they gonna split us up, but I won't be able to take Ferdie. I couldn't stand that, Dave."

Brandon straightened, as though trying to will away tears. But he failed.

"I'll call her," David said, putting an arm around him and offering him his handkerchief. Brandon leaned into him. "We'll see what we can work out."

Brandon blew his nose and drew a steadying breath, the brief display of emotion over. "I mean it about the money. You can have it all if we can stay here."

"We're brothers," David said squeezing his shoulder, "not business partners in a corporation. You don't have to offer me a better deal to stay on. You're welcome here."

"And Ferdie?"

"Ferdie, too."

"What if the lady doesn't like it?"

David laughed. "How could anybody not like you guys?"

"Mom doesn't," Brandon said.

"Mom's got problems," David reminded him.

"I've told you that before. She doesn't like being a mother like most other women do."

"Then why did she have three children?"

That was such a practical question, David wished he had a more sensible answer than, "Because she needs something she can't find. She looks for it in husbands and boyfriends, and when she was younger, if she thought they were going to leave, she had a baby, thinking it would make them stay. But they left anyway and there she is."

Brandon socked him in the side. "Anyway. I'm glad she had you, or Brady and I would be in deep...you know."

"Yeah. Come on, let's call her. She's probably worried."

"Yeah," Brandon said, keeping up with him as they walked toward the kitchen, Ferdie following. "The trust fund escaped. Darby wants her to put him in charge of it so he can get into it. But I want you to have it."

David groaned privately as he guided Brandon and Ferdie toward the main stairway. After all, it wasn't every day that a man was called upon to find the mother of his unborn child, help her sister, who was so upset she couldn't identify her own face in a mirror, make a home amid the chaos of his life for two prepubescent brothers while turning down two point seven million dollars.

God. Had Brandon really seen Gusty? And if he had, where was she going? And who was the scary-looking man with her?

ATHENA MADE THE CALL from the kitchen and waited impatiently while someone went in search of Officer Holden. It was only as her eyes roved the room that she realized something was cooking. A wonderful aroma caught her attention.

She was just focusing on that, trying to determine what it was and how it had gotten here while she and David had been gone most of the day, when a short, plump woman with curly gray hair came in through the back door. She clutched a handful of what looked like parsley.

She started at the sight of Athena, but Brady walked into the room at the same moment.

"Dotty!" he shouted, and ran to her. She put the parsley on the counter and wrapped him in plump arms.

She was not much taller than he was. "Well, Brady," she said, squeezing him tightly. "You're back earlier than expected. Where's Brandon?"

Brady tipped his head toward the living room. "He's 'making a deal' with Dave."

"A deal?"

"He thinks he has to offer him money to keep us. He's been around Mom too long."

The woman looked over Brady's head at Athena a little regretfully, as though embarrassed they'd shared a family secret in front of strangers.

"Mom and Darby want to send us to separate boarding schools," Brady explained to Dotty. "And Brandon wouldn't be able to bring Ferdie."

"Ferdie?"

"Our dog."

Dotty smoothed his hair, her mouth curving ruefully. "I don't suppose it's a small dog?"

"No. He's a bunch of different kinds, but he's really big." He related the story about Ferdie going to the pound. "But if he gets this kitchen muddy, I'll clean it up so you won't have to."

Dotty kissed his forehead. "That's my boy."

"Officer Holden," a voice said suddenly in Athena's ear.

"Oh! Officer!" Athena realized she was shouting and lowered her voice. "This is Athena Ames. I think my sister's been spotted at the Portland airport!" She told him everything Brandon had told them, and gave him the description of the man who'd accompanied her. "The boys' flight came in at 12:35 this afternoon."

"That'll help." He sounded less enthused than she'd hoped. "Can you bring them by in the morning to talk to me?"

"David isn't here right now, but yes, I think so. Do you think this means we'll find her?"

"It'll help, Miss Ames," he said again.

"But..." She wanted him to tell her it meant he could *find* Gusty. "Now we know where she was just a few hours ago."

She realized as she said those words that what they really needed to know was where she was right now. So, she'd flown into Portland. All they had to do was find her among five hundred thousand people.

"He said the man was scary looking," she added lamely, her throat thickening.

"We'll check passenger lists on Northwest flights

arriving at that time,'' he said, his tone a little more encouraging. ''We'll find her.''

''But she doesn't remember her name. She won't be listed that way.''

''We might be able to spot an alias. Or maybe a cab driver will remember them. Or one of the airport employees. We'll see you tomorrow, then?''

''Yes. Thank you, Officer.'' She hung up the phone, her excitement of a few moments ago deflating.

Dotty came to her. ''Hello, Athena,'' she said, taking her hands. ''I'm Dotty Jones, David's housekeeper. Brady just told me about your sister, and don't you worry. David will help you find her. I've been with him since he set out on his own, you know. Followed him here from Chicago. Used to work for his mother.'' She rolled her eyes descriptively. ''But that's another story. So, you're a houseguest, I understand. I've been away with friends for a few days.''

''Ah, yes.'' That welcome helped Athena push her worries aside. She looked at the smiling boy and remembered she wasn't the only one with problems here. ''Thank you, Dotty. I hope I didn't frighten you.''

''Course not!'' She laughed lightly. ''You keep house for men long enough and nothing frightens you.''

''What can I do to help?''

Dotty handed her a stack of clean towels on the edge of the counter. ''Would you take these to the upstairs bathroom for me, please? And while you're up there, could you get an extra blanket for each of the boys out of the linen closet?''

''Of course.''

''You come down when you've got your things put away, Brady, and I'll give you something to keep you going until dinner. Six-thirty, as usual.''

Brady beamed. ''I'm glad you're here, Dotty.''

Brady's room looked down on the driveway. ''I like to watch the cars come and go,'' he explained to Athena as he dropped his pack on the bed.

When she'd been a child, Athena remembered, it had been an empty bedroom where she and her sisters played dress-up. They would look down on the driveway and pretend they were waiting for the arrival of the coach that would take them to the ball.

Brady unloaded the meager contents of his backpack—an extra pair of jeans, a very wrinkled sweatshirt, a couple of pairs of socks and underwear, and some kind of handheld electronic game.

Athena got him the extra blanket and placed it on the foot of his bed.

He hung his jacket, his jeans, and his sweatshirt in the closet, and studied them dangling there in the middle of nothing and seemed very satisfied with it.

He went to the window and looked down. ''I'm going to be a mechanic when I grow up,'' he said. ''And I'll be able to fix anything.''

''We could have used you yesterday.'' Athena told him about her accident.

He frowned knowingly. ''Too much speed and power in the turn.''

''Is this cool or what?'' Brandon asked, standing

in the doorway as he looked around him. Ferdie sniffed the air. "We're back for good. He says we can stay if it's okay with Mom."

Brady followed him to his room across the hall. It overlooked the ocean.

It was the room Lex used to occupy. Her sister used to set up her chalkboard by the window and draw the scene countless times, erasing it and drawing it again.

"Athena can get you an extra blanket," Brady told Brandon.

Athena went to do just that, and on second thought, retrieved two blankets—one for Ferdie, which she placed on the floor by the bed.

Brandon seemed to appreciate the gesture. "Thank you," he said. "Here, Ferdie. This is for you."

The dog approached, sniffed the blanket, turned in a circle and lay down. Brandon patted him affectionately. "Good boy."

The dog accepted the praise, then stretched out, prepared to rest now that he'd gotten his charges safely to their destination.

"Dotty said to come down when you're ready—" Athena backed out of the room "—and she'll give you something to nibble on until dinner."

Brandon nodded. "Thank you for the blankets."

She smiled, relating to the lost look in his eyes. "You're welcome."

David was on the phone in the kitchen when Athena walked in.

"I know, I know," he was saying placatingly, "but they were upset about the dog, and let's face it, Jordana, you're not that available for sharing grievances. Congratulations on your wedding, by the way.''

He sent Athena a dry glance, then turned to the window near where he stood. The sky was darkening to dusk.

Athena was suddenly filled with a heavy melancholy.

Dotty stood across the room, stirring something on the stove, and David, deep in the crisis that had brought his brothers to him, seemed to have retreated to a family place Athena knew very little about.

She hadn't realized until that moment how much she'd counted on his warmth and his openness the past few days. And now that there was *some* news on Gusty, she might very well have to pursue it alone.

She went to the cupboard for dishes and began to set the table, looking for a sense of being needed, of belonging. Now that she'd seen David with his brothers, every concern she'd ever had that he might have cheated or hurt her aunt vanished.

''Of course it was thoughtless,'' he said quietly. ''Yes, I imagine you were beside yourself.''

Dotty turned at that to catch his eye and they shared a moment of what appeared to be wry amusement.

''No,'' he said. ''They're fine here for a while. Yes, I know they should. Dancer's Beach has a great school they share with the neighboring town.'' David listened for a few moments.

Athena could hear what sounded like a lengthy, high-pitched protest to that suggestion.

''Look, Jordana,'' he said finally. ''All they have is each other, and you want to send them to separate schools. And you know Brandon can't have the dog there. Why would you do that to them?''

More high-pitched argument on the other end of the line.

''Yeah, but they're not ready for college yet, so it's a little early for the right prep school. They're just young boys who—'' he seemed to be picking his words carefully ''—aren't really comfortable in your present circumstances, and would be happier here for a while. Why don't we give it a try? Sure. Ask Darby. I'll wait.''

Dotty stopped what she was doing to also await the answer.

Athena was surprised to find that it was important to her, too—though it presented a major kink in the solution of her problems.

''Okay,'' David said calmly after a moment. ''Why don't you ship some of their clothes and their favorite things, and I'll give you regular reports on how it's going.''

Dotty blew a kiss to heaven in gratitude, then went back to her cooking.

A thundering on the stairs marked the arrival of the boys just as David was hanging up the phone.

''Was that Mom?'' Brady asked.

David nodded.

''What'd she say?'' Brandon's eyes were hopeful.

''That I can enroll you in school here,'' David replied, ''and see how it goes.''

Brady let out a spirited ''yahoo!'' and leaped at David.

Athena watched David brace his stance to receive

him and thought it a pity Gusty's baby *wasn't* his. He had father potential written all over him.

"I can take out the garbage and mow the lawn," Brady bargained, apparently taking seriously his brother's philosophy about "dealing" for what you wanted.

"That'd work," David said, setting him down. "Though you won't have to worry about the lawn with fall coming."

Brady pointed to the apple trees in the backyard. "Pretty soon there'll be lots of leaves to rake. When they're gone I can help Dotty with the dishes." That figured out, Brady went across the kitchen to check out dinner.

Brandon looked as though the weight of a truck had been removed from his shoulders. "Thanks, Dave." David, apparently trying to keep the moment as simple as Brandon wanted it, just nodded. "Sure."

"And it's okay to have Ferdie in the house? He doesn't piddle, or anything."

"It is."

David patted Brandon's shoulder. "You'd better come with me to pick up some dog food. You can show me what Ferdie likes. You need anything, Dotty?"

She smiled at him across the kitchen. "Got everything under control." She gave Brady a peach and tossed one at Brandon. "Here you go. This'll keep you going until dinner."

"Dinner looks great!" Brady reported. "Chicken and roasted potatoes and…well, vegetables, but you can't have everything. Can I come to the store, too?"

"Sure. Come on." David turned to Athena. "You need anything?"

She shook her head. "Thanks. I'm fine. When I talked to Officer Holden, he wanted to know if you'd bring the boys to talk to him tomorrow."

He handed Brandon the car keys. "You guys okay with talking to the police about the woman you saw at the airport?"

They nodded simultaneously. "But we told you everything," Brandon said.

David nodded. "He'd probably like to hear it directly from you. Go sit in the car, but don't drive off."

As the boys raced each other out the door, laughing at that suggestion, David went to Athena. He looked into her face, clearly trying to read her mood after the event at the store and the recent discovery about Gusty. "You're sure you're fine?"

She felt a little ripple of pleasure that with all he had to have on his mind at this moment, he was concerned about her state of mind and her feelings.

She nodded. "I'm very resilient."

"Did Holden say anything else?"

"He said he can check passenger lists and airport employees who might remember them, but he could have just been humoring me."

He put a hand to her arm and stroked gently. "Sounds like a good clue to me. And don't worry about the boys being here slowing down the search. We'll find her."

"They're going to need you," she replied. "Maybe I should just—"

"I'll be here, don't forget," Dotty interrupted, forming biscuits in her hands and dropping them onto a cookie sheet. "You two can do whatever it is you're doing. And the boys will be in school during the day."

David turned to Athena, arms out in a broad "that's settled" gesture. "We'll do it together. And I wouldn't worry too much about the 'scary-looking man' remark. You know kids. He might have just been concentrating and looked hostile to Brandon."

A million questions crowded her brain. Then who was he? And where was he taking Gusty? But David had other things to do right now, so she kept them to herself.

"Okay. Thanks."

The sound of a horn honking invaded from the driveway, the boys apparently growing impatient.

David closed his eyes and shook his head. "This is going to be such fun. Be back in time for dinner."

"You better be," Dotty said sweetly, "or Athena and I are polishing this off ourselves. And there's pumpkin pie for dessert."

"I wouldn't want to be you," David grinned as he opened the back door, "when you tell the boys there's no dessert. We won't be long."

The moment the door closed behind him, Athena excused herself to Dotty and went upstairs to call Patrick and apprise him of the new situation.

Chapter Eight

Everyone pitched in with dishes and cleaning up after dinner, then Dotty made a fresh pot of decaf before retiring for the night.

"You're going to Astoria tomorrow?" she asked David. He looked the boys over. Their clothes were wrinkled and smudged.

"We'll see Officer Holden, then we'll take the boys to the mall for a couple of changes of clothes until their things get here. I'll enroll them the day after."

"Then breakfast at eight as usual?"

"Great."

"All right, then. See you all in the morning."

Dotty disappeared into her room off the kitchen and the boys wanted to know if they could watch the big-screen television in the family room.

"Okay." David glanced at his watch. "Bed at ten o'clock. But only until we get you into school, then it's nine."

Neither boy seemed inclined to complain as he ran off.

David walked with Athena into the living room.

Athena gathered up the bags filled with her new

clothing that the boys had carried in from the car for her when they'd returned from the market.

She'd done her best not to think about Gusty and to concentrate on the boys, who seemed eager to talk. She knew David had other things to deal with now. And she was plagued with guilt over the fact that Gusty's absence really *wasn't* his problem.

Having seen him in action with his brothers, she was now completely convinced he'd had nothing to do with her aunt's disappearance. She had to explain about the night of the costume party—but how did they account for all the interrelated mysteries still left dangling?

How had her aunt known him and why did she leave him the house?

What had her sister been doing on the Oregon coast seven months' pregnant? And who was the man with her?

And how in the name of all that was holy, was she going to explain that she'd once considered him responsible for all of it, crashed his party, then let him believe her sister was pregnant with his baby?

''I'll help you with that,'' David said, taking two of the larger bags from her. ''Don't worry about Gusty. We'll find her.''

''I don't know,'' she said wearily, preceding him up the stairs. ''We know a little something now, but it's almost more frightening than it was before.''

Distracted, she stumbled on the stairs and slid down against the balusters to land on her backside.

David, arms full of her packages, couldn't react quickly enough.

She groaned at her own clumsiness as he sank down beside her, tossing the packages aside.

"Are you all right?" he asked, hands going to her arms to pull her upright. "It looked like you bumped your ribs on the stair."

"I did, but it's carpeted and soft. I'm fine." She brushed herself off. "I don't seem to be able to drive or walk while I'm thinking about—" She stopped abruptly because he was staring at her with a frown, his eyes roving her face with an intensity that sent a ripple of alarm along her spine. Did he know? she wondered breathlessly. Did he know she was "Constance" and not Augusta?

She waited, heart pounding, for him to confront her with the accusation.

Instead, he smiled suddenly and put a hand to her cheek. It was all she could do not to close her eyes and lean into the touch. But she suspected he didn't even know he was doing it.

"It's a stupid thing to say when you've told me you're identical twins." He withdrew his hand and sighed. "But you're so much like her. Your face when you were laughing reminded me of that night. We were sitting right about here on the stairs, eating food from the buffet and drinking champagne."

It was her opportunity to say "I know. It *was* me!" But she couldn't do it. She could see the cherished memory in his eyes and remembered his words about her being the most wonderful woman he'd ever met, and she just couldn't kill that moment—for him or for herself.

"You did?" she whispered.

"Yeah," he said. "I think I was already in love at that point."

In love. She couldn't move, couldn't think.

He pushed himself to his feet, then reached down to help her to hers. He scooped up the bags and followed her to her room.

"I'm sorry about this afternoon," he said abruptly from the doorway.

She turned from spilling out the contents of the bags onto the bed, trying to behave naturally when her brain refused to function.

"In the dressing room," he clarified. "I forgot that you weren't her." He leaned a shoulder in the doorway and braced a hand against the other side. "I don't know why it happened. I guess it's because you're so identical. I'd have thought that I would connect only with Gusty and not with someone who looks just like her, but I seem…" He shook his head, clearly unable to explain his feelings.

She came halfway toward him, preparing to try to explain, but he went on. "I didn't want you to think I was trying to take advantage of your emotional vulnerability under the circumstances."

"David…"

"I was with her so briefly, and the part of our union that was the most important, I don't even remember and I really regret that. I hate that she lived for months probably wondering why I hadn't called and come to see her."

"No, I—"

"Dave!" There were pounding footsteps along the

hall, then Brady appeared. "Are there cookies in the cookie jar on top of the refrigerator?"

"Yes," David replied. "But you just had dinner. And seconds."

"That was an hour ago," Brady replied seriously.

David grinned. "How true. Help yourself."

"I can't reach it. But I can stand on a chair!"

David caught the back of Brady's shirt as the boy would have left to put the plan to work. "Wait. I'll get it down for you." To Athena, he added, "You're welcome to come downstairs with us. You don't have to stay up here."

"Thanks," she demurred, "but I've got to put my things away. Maybe I'll just read for a while and turn in early."

"You'll be missing out on cookies," he teased.

She held up a pair of jeans. "I have new clothes that have to fit until we find Gusty."

"All right. Good night." He reached for the doorknob. "Door open or closed?"

"Closed, please. Good night, Brady."

"Good night, Athena."

Athena put her clothes away, took a shower, climbed into bed and lay drowsily against her pillows. She was just about to drift off when her cell phone rang.

It was Patrick. "Hey, Red. How's it going?"

She sat up. Unable to answer that in one concise sentence, she evaded, "All right. What have you got? Tell me it's news about Gusty."

"No, I'm sorry. I'm working on it, though. But I do have something on your guys."

She swallowed disappointment to concentrate on what he had found. "What is it?"

"Well," he replied, "I thought maybe if I started fresh that I'd spot something I'd missed when we did this in February."

"Yeah? And did you?"

"No." He sounded confused. "There's nothing. Their personal stuff and their employment information is available. But they sort of disappear every once in a while without a trace. No travel information, no car rentals, no motel rooms."

She frowned over that, confused herself. "So what does that mean?"

"I don't know. Unless..."

"Unless what?"

"They're not CIA or something, are they? Nobody covers their tracks and makes time disappear like they do."

She remembered suddenly the careful way David talked about his past, the "investigative" work he'd done that had taught him to handle stress, the friend who was lost in one particular investigation. But he'd called Sadie a co-worker.

"Oh, my God!" she whispered. "If that's it, what does it have to do with my aunt?"

"I don't know, Athena," he said. "I checked Sadie out to see if their paths had crossed and it's the damnedest thing."

Athena's throat went dry. "What?"

"She disappears at exactly the same times they do."

She gasped.

"Last year her mail was held for three weeks."

"She went to Greece," Athena put in quickly.

"In April, not in September. And the year before, she was gone in March and July—same time the men were missing."

"She took cruises."

"No, she didn't. She booked but never showed."

"I don't understand!" she whispered urgently.

Patrick cleared his throat, as though unwilling to pass on his thoughts. "I'd say if those guys were spooks," he said, "it's possible Sadie was, too."

Athena didn't know what else to say, so she simply said, "Thanks, Pat."

"Sure. I'll stay on it and be in touch."

She turned off the phone and sank into her pillows, more confused than ever. Aunt Sadie was a spy?

Athena felt as though the world had fallen away under her feet.

HOLDEN QUESTIONED THE BOYS kindly but thoroughly, and it was clear they'd noticed nothing more than they'd told David.

"Did the man say anything?" Holden asked. "Did you hear his voice? Was it loud? Soft? Did he have an accent?"

Brandon shook his head. "No. I just noticed that he was grumpy looking."

"Was he grumpy to the woman?"

"No, he was nice to her. He told her to sit in a chair while he got the bags."

"Yeah!" Brady added. "But he kept watching her, like he thought she might run away."

David saw Athena's brow furrow worriedly.

"That could have been concern," he said, as much to convince himself as to comfort her.

"Okay, I think that's it." Holden ushered them through the busy front office to the door. "Thanks for coming all this way. I'll let you know when we turn up anything."

David saw Brandon elbow Brady. "Why did you have to say that?" he whispered harshly.

"Because it was true!" Brady replied.

David put a hand on each boy's shoulder. "You guys did fine. Let's go get some lunch, then we'll get your clothes." He put them into the back of the car, then put a hand to Athena's arm when she tossed her purse into the front.

"We have to stay hopeful," he said firmly. "If this guy had intended to hurt her, he'd have done it already."

"Then why doesn't he just take her home?" she asked, her eyes troubled.

"Maybe he doesn't know who she is, either."

"Or maybe he's the reason she ended up in the river in the first place. And he went and got her at the hospital so she won't talk."

He tightened his grip on her arm and gave her a small shake. "We don't know that her fall into the river was anything more than an accident, and if he didn't want her to talk, she'd be gone already. He wouldn't have taken her out into a crowd at the airport."

She looked into his eyes and he saw that she wanted to believe him. She held his gaze for a moment, then sighed. "Yeah, maybe," she said, and got into the car.

He closed her door, doing his best to believe his own scenario.

ATHENA SERVED AS GOFER while the boys tried on school clothes, fetched and carried while they were in the dressing rooms, getting bigger or smaller sizes, different colors, "cooler" styles.

It was midafternoon before each boy had three changes of clothes he could live with. Shoes took another hour.

They stopped in a stationery story for notebooks, paper and pens.

"Can I have graph paper?" Brady asked. "I love graph paper. I'm going to design things when I'm a grown-up."

David found it on the shelf and handed him a pack.

"I thought you were going to be a mechanic," Brandon said.

"Yeah," Brady replied. "A mechanic who designs things."

Brandon frowned at David. "Is there such a thing?"

David shrugged. "Maybe he'll be a first. You got everything you need?"

"I guess. Know what I'm going to be?"

"You don't have to be anything." Brady looked lustfully at a plastic bubble pack that contained a ruler, a protractor, a compass and several erasers. "You have your trust fund. Can I have this, too?"

"Yes." David handed one to Brandon, also.

"Brady, you don't work just to make money. You pick a career because it makes you feel good to do whatever it is you do. What are you going to be, Brand?"

"A screenwriter." Brandon looked momentarily embarrassed by the admission. Then he shrugged and said, as though he couldn't help it, "I see stories in my head all the time." He laughed suddenly. "Mom thinks it means I'm hearing voices and wants me to go to a shrink. Only Darby thought it'd embarrass everybody, so she didn't make the appointment."

David laughed, too. It amazed him that such a self-ish and clueless woman could have produced his interesting and intelligent brothers.

"That's great." David pushed their cart toward the Office Shops counter. "What kind of screenplays? Mysteries? Science fiction?"

"I have an idea for a detective story, but I haven't had a chance to write any of it down yet. Darby's always on the computer doing that day trading thing."

David pulled things out of the cart and placed them on the counter. Brady dragged Athena to a display of desk accessories while the clerk rang up their purchases.

"You can use my computer." David handed the clerk his credit card. "I'm not going to get much done while we're looking for Athena's sister."

"That'd be cool." Brandon took the heavy sack the clerk handed across the counter.

Athena and Brady came up behind them while David signed the credit card transmittal. She carried two large plastic desk organizers in bright colors.

David tried to take them from her and add them on to his purchase, but she held them away from him.

"No, these are my gift to the boys." She dropped them on the counter and gave the clerk her bank card.

"Guys," Brady whispered loudly. "Not boys. That sounds wimpy. We're guys."

"Sorry. Guys," she amended.

David drove by the Matthew Buckley School on the way home. The boys pressed their faces to the window. It was dusk and all the children had long since left the playground. "I wonder if the kids are smarter than us?" Brandon said.

"Some probably are," David replied, "and some aren't. Everybody's different."

"The determination to learn," Athena said, "is more important than your IQ. My sister had trouble in school and now she's a brilliant art—" She stopped, her heart pounding. What had she almost said?

She'd almost said that her sister was an artist, when David thought she had only one sister and that she was a teacher.

Everyone waited for her to finish.

"Art teacher," she said, plumping out the story to provide a distraction. "She had a lot of trouble with art, but as a third-grade teacher she has to help the children with it, so she studied hard and now her students do really good work."

"Little kids just do really easy artwork," Brady, a

fifth-grader, pointed out. She was tempted to bean him with his desk organizer.

"But she probably still has to teach them the principles," David said, "so she has to have studied well to know them."

"Oh."

Athena could have kissed David for swallowing her story and negating the importance of Brady's observation.

And for a distracting moment, kissing him was more than simply a passing thought.

She remembered his lips on hers that night of the party and, if she concentrated, she could feel them now. Warm, supple, clever.

She had to give herself a shake when she discovered they were home and everyone was waiting in front of the parked car, staring through the windshield at her, wondering what was keeping her.

She hurried to join them.

She had intended to find an opportunity after dinner that night to ask David directly about Sadie and to tell him the truth about her own identity, but he and the boys got involved on the computer when he explained to Brandon the workings of the word processing program, and she finally said good-night and went to bed.

She awoke at ten minutes after two in the morning feeling rested and decidedly hungry.

Remembering the delicious ham Dotty had served for dinner, she thought a half sandwich might be just the thing to help her back to sleep. Tomorrow they were taking the boys to school, then retracing their steps north in their continuing search for Gusty. And on the way, she would talk to him as she'd planned.

She didn't bother with a robe, since the house was quiet, and tiptoed downstairs in her bare feet, headed for the kitchen.

DAVID HAD LAIN AWAKE for hours, trying to think things through. He decided he could just about put an end to his plans for a quiet new life as a writer.

With the recent discovery that he was about to become a father, and the possibility that his brothers were going to become a permanent part of his daily life, quiet was out of the question.

How would Gusty feel about helping him raise two adolescent boys? he wondered. Then he realized there was no point in worrying about that until he had some clue how she felt about *him*.

And just to confuse the situation, all the time he thought about Gusty, it was Athena's face he pictured. But they were identical sisters, so it was all right, wasn't it?

He had an unsettling feeling it wasn't, and that was what was keeping him awake. Women weren't interchangeable—even identical twins. However much she might resemble her twin, inside she was different.

He remembered the woman he'd sat with the night of the party and thought she'd seemed less guarded than Athena was. He always got the impression Athena didn't entirely trust him.

She was good with the boys, though, and didn't seem at all upset that they'd delayed their search for Gusty. She seemed to like Dotty, had been...more than warm with him in the dressing room at Your Neck of the Woods.

God. He hoped this mess would be settled soon. When he and Gusty were under the same roof and Athena was back in D.C., he'd be sane again.

Maybe.

Also worrisome was the e-mail he'd gotten tonight from his old features editor. "Dave," it had said. "Just wanted to let you know that someone's asking about you, been into the *Trib*'s employee records, trying to find out where you went when you and Mc-Ginty took vacations. What's going on? You made some enemies? Thought you should know. Sam."

Great. Just what the current mix needed. A threat to his personal safety at a time when his house was filled with vulnerable guests.

David climbed out of bed and went downstairs in the T-shirt and tailored blue pajama bottoms he slept in. He'd bring up a brandy and write until he felt sleepy.

He was halfway across the living room when he heard the noise. It was a very small sound—just a sigh of air as someone moved almost silently in the kitchen.

He remembered Sam's e-mail. The thought of the boys and Athena upstairs, and Dotty only yards away off the kitchen, brought back the fighting edge he'd been trying to shed for the past few months. It pumped in his blood, sang through his veins, steadied his breath and his control to prepare every muscle in his body.

He moved into and across the dining room as

though it were booby-trapped, then stood still and listened.

The smallest of sounds was coming his way. He took one lateral step to use the concealment of the doorway just as a shadow moved through it.

He judged its shape and pounced.

He caught a throat in the crook of his arm, and the other encircled a waist. There was an instant of quiet surprise, then whatever he held came off the floor and turned into an armload of piranha.

Teeth sank into his arm and worked it like an ear of corn. Fingernails ripped at the side of his face, heels kicked at his shins, and all the while threats of crippling injury so pervasive even his grandchildren would be affected were screamed at him in a high, furious voice. Something whipped at his face. Hair. Long, fragrant hair...

Even as he tipped his intruder sideways and onto the floor in an attempt to save himself from further injury, he recognized the voice—and the hair.

And in the blur of the moment, a nebulous truth almost came together in his mind. But the writhing woman in his arms wouldn't allow him to focus. He tried to chase the thought, knowing only that something wasn't quite right. The kitchen light went on suddenly, and Dotty stood there, a butcher knife raised menacingly.

Then all the other downstairs lights went on and the boys raced into the dining room, Brandon wielding his bat, Brady following. Ferdie ran ahead of them, barking ferociously.

When the dog caught sight of David, he stopped in confusion, turning to Brandon, awaiting instructions.

''What's going on?'' the boy demanded at the same moment that Dotty shouted, ''Sakes alive, what *happened?*''

His mind still half at work on the important equation that refused to form for him, David looked down at Athena, her back pinned by his knee, her legs kicking for all she was worth. Her hair, hanging loose, had parted in the back and concealed her face, but exposed her back and shoulders in the silky black sliplike nightgown.

He saw a small scar on the ridge of her shoulder and the answer came to him with the impact of a blow to the head.

ATHENA WAS SURE David's knee was going to break her back. The moment the lights went on and she recognized the pajama bottoms, she knew the viselike arm had to belong to David. Not that she'd seen him in pajamas, but she couldn't imagine that an intruder would have broken in dressed in nightwear.

''I woke up hungry,'' she said, her voice strained because of her facedown position. ''I was making a...a sandwich.''

''Here it is!'' Brandon's voice said. ''Ferdie found it.''

It sounded as though he was also eating it.

Mercifully, Athena was lifted to her feet. She brushed the hair out of her face and smiled a little shamefacedly at Dotty, who came close to touch her cheek diagnostically.

"Are you all right?" the housekeeper asked. "It sounded like combat down here."

Athena drew a deep breath. Her ribs might be bruised but they weren't broken. "I think I'm fine," she said, suddenly finding the humor in the situation. "I guess David must have heard me, and thought I was..."

She'd turned to look up at David as she spoke and stopped short when she saw the look on his face.

"A burglar," she finished lamely.

This time he did know. She had no idea how he'd found out, but something about that skirmish had told him the truth. Oh, God.

"Cool!" Brandon came forward with his bat. "I'm glad it was you, 'cause I'm really not much of a hitter."

She wanted to die. And that was probably good, because David looked as though he would be happy to accommodate her at the earliest possible moment.

"Why were you making a sandwich in the dark?" he asked on a cool, deadly note.

"I'd already made the sandwich and I was leaving when I realized I didn't have my cup of tea. So I went back to get it, had to grope around the counter for it and...I don't know where it went."

"Over here." Brandon picked the empty cup off the floor near the window. "The carpet's all wet."

"Not to worry, it'll blot right up." Dotty turned to get paper towels and pressed them onto the spot.

David urged the boys back to bed, then let Dotty put fresh towels on the stain and told her to go back to bed, that the job could be finished in the morning.

"But it's tea," she complained.

"In the morning," he insisted quietly. "Good night, Dotty."

The housekeeper looked from David to Athena and seemed to catch the sudden tension. She studied them a moment, then said good-night and walked away.

David pointed Athena in the direction of the conservatory. She went, noting absently that he was gorgeous in a temper. The symmetrical line of his features was undisturbed by his usual animation so that she saw straight eyebrows above an even stare, lips set in an unyielding slash, jaw tight and square. Shoulders like a stone wall between her and escape.

He turned on one small light on the wicker table behind the sofa. He slapped the back of a sofa cushion and ordered, "Sit down."

She complied, more regretful than afraid. But her hands were shaking.

She usually loved this room filled with green plants of every description sitting on tables, on stands, in wrought iron racks and hanging from tall, decorative posts. But there was nothing welcoming and friendly about it at that moment.

"Where'd you get the scar?" he asked.

She turned to look at him over her shoulder, startled by what seemed like an irrelevant question. "What scar?"

"This one." His index finger swiped over a spot on her neck where it curved into her shoulder. She got a toaster-in-the-bathwater sort of feeling. She kept it to herself, knowing the last thing he was aware of at the moment was sexual tension.

"Oh," she said, putting her hand to it. He'd already removed his. "I fell against a glass-top coffee table as a child."

But she knew that answer wasn't the point of his question.

"I felt it the night we made love." He came around the sofa to sit on the chair facing it. He leaned back, his arms on the arms of the chair like some plantation boss. "Why did you lie to me?"

"I didn't lie to you," she disputed. "*You* told me you'd made love to Gusty."

That handsome, angry face hardened further. "Don't split hairs with me, Athena. I'm in no mood."

"I'm just trying to make sure," she said, "that you remember things correctly."

"I remember that I made love to you."

She sighed and rubbed her arms. The glassed-in room was cold, despite the temperate weather. "You didn't make love to me. You went to sleep."

He stared at her, obviously unwilling to believe that. "I remember…"

"Then you're remembering your plans to make love to me," she said insistently, "or you dreamed that you did, and that's what you recall. You did not make love to me." She looked down at her flat tummy in the skimpy nightie and asked, arms outspread, "Do I look pregnant?"

Judging by the sudden pain and disappointment on his face, that was the first moment he realized what this meant. He was not about to become a father. Someone else had made love to Gusty. He seemed to need a moment to adjust to that. She stood by helplessly as sadness crossed his expression. Then the anger returned.

"What was your point," he asked finally, "in letting me believe Gusty carried *my* baby."

"Because," she replied intrepidly, meeting his eyes, "you were willing to help me look for her. And finding her is one of the most important things in my life."

He absorbed that, then shook his head and asked in disbelief, "And it never occurred to you that was a cruel thing to do to someone?"

She closed her eyes, knowing he was going to love this part, still there was nothing else to do but get it over with.

"At first I thought you were the father of Gusty's baby. I mean, we were all wearing masks the night of the ball, and I—"

"All?" He frowned. "You mean, she was at the house, too?"

"Yes." It had been on the tip of her tongue to say, "We all were," and explain Lexie, as well, but she decided at the last moment that her lie of omission about a third sister was not what the moment needed, not if she didn't intend to alienate him altogether. "Gusty was here, too."

"Why?"

She raised her hands, palms up, to encompass the room in which they sat. "Gusty and I spent our childhoods here. Sadie Richmond was our aunt."

"What?"

She ignored his darkening brow and plunged on. "She had always promised to leave us the house because it had been in our family for years and she knew we loved it. She had no children of her own. Then her plane crashes, her lawyer reads the will, and we discover that she left it to you!''

She could see the anger and hostility deepening in his eyes as he misinterpreted her motives.

''Our concern had nothing to do with getting the house for ourselves!'' she snapped at him. ''It had to do with some guy forcing her out of her home. We thought you might have coerced her into it, or something, so we came to the party to talk to you and your friends and try to find out what happened.''

''So you came to my home,'' he said, in the nature of an accusation, ''pretending to be someone else.''

''We were in costume,'' she reminded. ''Everyone was pretending to be someone else.''

He let several seconds tick away. ''I warned you about splitting hairs.''

''Yes, you did.'' She got to her feet and paced the width of the conservatory, rubbing her arms. ''But it seems to be required in the case of your selective memory. The way I recall it, I was standing near the stairs, and you were the one who approached me. So don't make it sound as though I cornered you and seduced you into talking.''

He remained calmly in his chair, watching her move across the room and back again. ''Did you find out anything incriminating?''

''I found out,'' she admitted candidly, ''that you're a kind and caring man, and I soon gave up on the notion that you'd have done anything to hurt Sadie.''

She saw surprise in his eyes, but he banked it instantly.

"But you continued to lie."

"I needed you to help me find Gusty."

"Whom you let me believe was carrying my baby."

"It made you more eager to find her." That was a little hard to admit, in view of how selfish and manipulative it sounded, but she did it anyway. "By the way, why did you brick up the door to the stairway that goes down to the beach?"

He measured her reason for asking that question before he replied. "Because the stairs were broken and slimy and I had two adolescent boys coming to visit me for a month. It seemed safer to make it inaccessible. Why? Did you think I was using it to transport blond virgins out to boats destined for slave markets in the Orient?"

She sighed. "Something like that."

He accepted that calmly, though a muscle worked in his jaw. "You said that each of you was supposed to find out why your aunt left me the house. So, which of my friends was Gusty with that night? Trevyn or Bram?"

"I don't know." She walked toward the windows. "The masks again. And the three of you were dressed the same. I wasn't sure who I was with, and, I guess, neither was she."

"So..." He got to his feet and yanked a fringed, brightly colored cotton throw off the back of the sofa and stood in her path as she started back toward him again. He folded it into a triangle. "How far would you have gone that night if I hadn't passed out?"

She stopped within several feet of him. He held the throw out to her.

She hesitated, her turn to be surprised. Then she accepted it and wrapped it around herself. "Thank you. I guess we'll never know. I had a lot at stake. My mother was a very poor parent, and Aunt Sadie was everything to us."

He considered that, then folded his arms. She couldn't decide if that was a good or bad sign.

"I take it Gusty didn't find out anything incriminating either that night. If her baby is the result of that encounter, she apparently wasn't mistrustful of my friend. Neither of them would have forced her to do anything she wasn't willing to do."

"There's no way of knowing, of course, without asking her," she said. "But Gusty isn't promiscuous. I can't believe she'd have made love with one of your friends, then gone home days later and made love again with someone else."

DAVID WAS TOO ANGRY to feel compassion for her. But it was easy to feel compassion for the pregnant woman out there somewhere who didn't know where to turn. And if that baby belonged to one of his friends, he had even more concern invested.

"I'll get a motel first thing in the morning," she said, "and continue the search on my own. Now that your brothers are here, you'll have a lot to occupy your time." She angled her chin and firmed her stance. "But first, I'd like to know why *you've* lied to *me*."

Convinced that question was a tactic to divert him from his anger and make him somehow responsible for what she'd done, he ignored it for a moment.

"Don't," he interrupted, "make my decisions for me. If anything turns me off a woman, it's that." And just to make certain she understood that he was angry and offended, he added, "That's second only to lying to me. And when in the hell did I ever lie to you?"

"You told me," she accused, "that you were an investigative reporter."

Okay. He guessed where this was going and he didn't like it. "That was the truth," he replied calmly.

"But not all of it." She shifted her weight.

He tried to ignore the shapely legs moving against the black silk.

"You weren't entitled to all of it," he argued quietly. "You were a stranger, and I have memories I don't like to deal with unless I'm forced."

"But I'm Sadie's niece!"

So, somehow she'd found out about Sadie's involvement in his life. "But I didn't know that," he reminded her, "until just a moment ago. You failed to mention your true purpose in crashing my party."

Something suddenly occurred to him. "You're the one looking into my file at the *Trib!*" he accused.

She looked defensive rather than guilty. "I asked my detective to do it. I wanted to know why Sadie left the house to a perfect stranger. Then when you turned up when Gusty was missing, well, I couldn't

figure out how it connected, except that you were involved both times.''

"Why didn't you just ask me?''

"Because I didn't think you'd tell me the truth!''

"Oh.'' He rolled his eyes. "As opposed to all the
truths you've told me.''

She looked temporarily at a loss. He enjoyed that
for a moment, then remembered that she'd lost the
woman who'd been like a mother to her. The woman
whose voice had mothered him and his friends with
encouragement and information.

"I'm sorry about Sadie,'' he said. "I'd never even
seen her face until I saw her photo in the newspaper.
To us she was just a voice on the phone or the radio.''

Athena sat on the wicker footstool, pulling the
shawl more tightly around her. Her eyes were dark
and sad.

"How did she get involved with the CIA, anyway?'' she asked. "It is the CIA?''

"It is.'' He shrugged. "I'm not sure. Rumor was
she'd loved an operative involved in the Bay of Pigs
in Cuba in the sixties. He died on the beach with
everybody else and she decided to take his place.
She'd been our contact for the past three years.''

She looked both mystified and hurt. "Why
wouldn't she have told us?''

He shook his head. "Probably the same reason I
keep most of that to myself. A lot of it's ugly. A lot
of it hurts.''

She looked sympathetic and accepting, though still
troubled. "But, if you'd never even seen her, why did
she leave you Cliffside?''

"Because I got her out of a dicey situation in Africa," he replied, glossing over the ugly details of machete-wielding rebels and a lone contact in a hut just half a mile from their advance. "I didn't even do it personally because I was too far away. I'd have never made it in time. But I sent a group of mercenaries in and got a helicopter to get them all out."

She gaped at him in disbelief. "My aunt Sadie?"

He grinned, remembering Sadie's voice. "She was one tough cookie with nerves of steel. She saved my hide more than once with calm directions and vital information. I proposed to her once, but she turned me down." He grinned. "Too bad. I think we'd have gotten on."

"Why didn't you come to the reading of the will?" she asked.

"I got the message from Pineau," he replied, "but I thought it was a mistake. I didn't know anyone named Sadie Richmond. We knew her only as Aunty. So I declined the invitation. Then he express-mailed me the document telling me what I'd inherited and a letter from Aunty—Sadie—telling me why. Then he told me what items in the house Sadie had left her family and asked me to ship them on to him."

Athena stood, her eyes miserable. "My aunt was a spy and didn't tell me. And my sister was going to have a baby and didn't tell me. Why does no one trust me?"

His expression was dry. "You mean, besides the fact that you lie?" He shook his head and said wearily, "It has nothing to do with you. Sadie wasn't supposed to tell anybody what she was doing. And

Gusty must have had her reasons. I'm sure they'll become clear when we find her.''

''That's something,'' she said wearily but with a sudden squaring of her shoulders, ''that's no longer your responsibility, since we know the baby isn't yours.''

He caught her arm through the shawl and pulled her back as she tried to walk around him. ''My friends mean as much to me as your sister means to you. And if your sister's baby belongs to one of them, I'm still committed to finding her. I can't reach either one right now to let him know what's happening, so the best I can do is act in his place. You're staying right here until this is settled.''

She lifted her chin stubbornly. ''Maybe I don't want to.''

He met her stare. ''Maybe that doesn't matter. Go to bed. We have a lot to do tomorrow.''

''If you think you can keep me here,'' she said, ''just so you can get your own back by bossing me around, you can forget it. I'm a lawyer. I'm surrounded by men who talk big. I'm not impressed.''

He went to the table to turn off the light.

''Does muscle impress you?'' he asked lightly, walking to the door. He stood by it, waiting for her. She seemed to think twice about answering that. Smart woman. He was that close to tossing her over his shoulder like a sack of onions and carrying her up to her bed.

She remained stubbornly where she stood. ''So you're bigger. Do you usually take advantage of that?''

"When other options are eliminated, yes."

She came toward him, the hem of her nightgown moving gracefully around her knees. He kept his eyes diverted from the nipples nicely outlined by her folded arms over the thin black silk.

"Before you consider doing that," she said, giving him a sidelong glance as she walked past him and toward the kitchen and the back stairs, "you might count the scratches you sustained earlier tonight."

"And you might remember," he called after her, "how quickly you ended up on the floor."

He heard her footsteps on the stairs and went into the living room to turn off the downstairs lights. God, what a night.

He was no longer a father-to-be. He was painfully disappointed about that. He'd really warmed to the idea.

His friends were like family, but it was time he started his own. It cheered him a little that Brandon and Brady were staying with him.

He drew a breath and realized that it cheered him a lot.

And there was something else on the plus side. He was a free spirit again. He no longer belonged to the woman he'd been so sure carried his baby.

The question was, did he want to pursue a woman who'd lied to him on numerous occasions and in several different ways?

He groaned as he headed for the stairs.

Because the answer was yes.

Chapter Nine

Athena could see that the boys were nervous about starting a new school. She could only imagine the anxieties involved in meeting classmates for the first time at that self-conscious stage of development.

She'd always thought it fortunate that she and her sisters had gone to the same school from kindergarten through high school. It was only when they chose different colleges to pursue their different goals that she realized what life was like without their companionship and support.

"There's a basic rule in relationships," she said to Brandon, trying to offer comfort as they walked into the noisy building. There were children everywhere. "If you're nice to people, they'll be nice to you. You'll have new friends in no time."

He looked at her as though she wore fangs and antennae.

"You don't know much about twelve-year-old boys, do you?" David asked quietly as they followed the boys into the school office. "There'll be a power struggle first, then they'll get to know each other and make friends. It's always scary to wonder if you'll measure up.''

''Girls,'' she replied, ''are so much more civilized.''

He raised an eyebrow. ''Really. I hadn't noticed that.''

She stood back, knowing she had no defense against his reference to the discovery he'd made during their encounter last night.

David introduced the boys to the office secretary, a warm, cheerful woman who then introduced each boy to a classmate already waiting to take him to his room.

David and Athena waved them off.

''Good luck, guys,'' David said. ''I'll pick you up.'' He turned to the secretary. ''What time?''

''Three o'clock,'' she said.

''Three o'clock,'' he repeated. ''Right out front.''

David and Athena left with a packet of information about the school and a bus schedule.

DAVID SAT IN THE CAR, his wrist on the steering wheel, trying to decide what his next step should be.

Athena, leaning as far away from him as she could in the passenger seat, gave him a stiff side-glance. She'd avoided him over breakfast, and when she hadn't been able to, she'd spoken to him briefly, pithily.

Which was fine with him. He was still angry.

But she looked pale and tired and that seemed to twist something in his gut.

"You want to have a cup of coffee before we go home?" he asked a little stiffly.

"No, thank you," she said with apparent disregard for what that conciliatory gesture had cost him. She turned slightly in his direction, her tone abrupt as though she'd been working up to this for some time. "I'll get a motel room today. I've been thinking about it. We can't do anything but wait to see what the police find out from the airline passenger lists. It'll be better all around—"

"We had this out last night," he interrupted, his sympathy for her strained. "If that baby belongs to Trevyn or Bram, I'm as involved in this as you are. So just take it easy. You're staying with me."

She sighed. "You know, for a relatively nice guy, you sometimes talk as though you've just been pulled out of a peat bog somewhere. What century are you from, anyway?"

"It's the natural reaction," he said, "of a man who's been lied to and maneuvered by a woman who turned his life upside down then wants to just walk away from the mess. That makes me long for the old days when women accepted a quieter role."

"Well, I'm *not* quiet," she said reasonably if a little emphatically. "I will never *be* quiet, so if that displeases you, why don't I just—"

"Why don't you just try to be quiet," he interrupted again, "before I tie you to the luggage rack. You're staying, and that's final, I don't care how Neanderthal you consider me. You started this."

"You're the one who came to Astoria and invited me to Cliffside!"

"That's because I thought you were alone with nowhere to go. I didn't know you made a habit of crashing people's parties and spying on them."

"Ha! You should talk about spying!"

He ran a hand over his face and put his key in the ignition. "Some relationship this is," he said.

"This was an alliance for the purpose of finding a missing person," she corrected distinctly. "This is not a relationship. A woman of the new millennium, and a Neanderthal cannot have a relationship."

"Please," he said. "We were meant to be together since that night of the party. But we're going to have to straighten out a lot of things before that happens."

She leaned toward him. "It's not going to happen," she said fiercely. "I'm telling you it's not going to happen, so don't even think about it."

He looked into her eyes, a sudden quiet wisdom in his. "You're afraid that you don't really have that woman in you, aren't you? That woman who was sweet and seductive and flirted with me."

"I know I don't," she said firmly, looking out the window. "I was acting."

"Maybe that was the real you. Maybe even you didn't know she was inside you. Why is that? Why do you suppress her?"

"I don't suppress her," she said. She was growing more concerned with his observations than she'd been with his anger. "She just doesn't belong here."

"Where?"

"In my life. In…the courtroom." She didn't want to say it, but it came out anyway. "In my family."

He looked at her over his arm, his eyes dark and

penetrating. "Why? Because that woman is competition for your mother? She's gone now. You can be who you are."

She sighed and leaned her head back against the rest. "This is who I am," she said, closing her eyes, remembering the curse of being the favored child of the mother she and her sisters couldn't love. She'd finally tried to turn off all winning ways, to be cool and detached so that her mother wouldn't like her. To her distress, her mother had admired those qualities. "My sisters…my sister's safety," she amended quickly, "means everything to me. There's no room for anything else."

"I think you're confused," he said, moving his arm to the back of the seat as he turned toward her, "between who you think you are, and who you really are."

She didn't want to talk about this anymore. She gave him the drop-dead look she'd learned from her mother. "You just said I've spent all our time together lying to you. How could you possibly know who I am?"

"Just clever, I guess." He cupped the back of her head under the neat knot of her hair. "I can bring her out," he said, his eyes roving her face with sudden and paralyzing intensity.

She swallowed, her pulse quickening. "I'm telling you she…she isn't there."

"Prove me wrong then," he challenged, and lowered his mouth to hers.

She didn't like to think about her mother, but she tried to hold on to her image because it sometimes worked for her in the courtroom. When she knew that success for her client depended upon her giving no quarter, her ruthless pursuit of the facts, her unwillingness to concede anything for the outcome she wanted, she imagined her mother's impenetrable coolness and tried to put it into her own features.

As his mouth met hers, she rested her hands on his shoulders because there was no place else to put them, thinking that she could prove by her complete lack of reaction that she was right and he was wrong.

And it would have worked if he'd come on passionately with hot kisses and confining arms. It was easy to hold out against power.

Charm, however, was something else.

Apparently he had no intention of forcing out this woman he was so certain she suppressed, but to coax her out with teasing little kisses, with nibbles on her bottom lip, with nuzzles and nudges.

For a woman starved for such attention, she put up a valiant struggle. She remained stiff and impassive. Until he planted a kiss in the hollow of her throat and she gasped at the exquisite touch.

Then he took advantage of that moment to invade her mouth with more determination, to explore and cajole and lure from her the reaction she tried so hard to withhold.

It rose out of her like fireworks—the kind that appear to be one colorful but simple explosion, then explode again into half a dozen brilliant bursts.

She was aware first of leaning into him, of making the most of that invasive kiss, and as she felt his hands move on her back—caressing her, drawing her closer—of her hands framing his face and taking control.

ONE PART OF DAVID'S AWARENESS was surprised by the ardor of her response. He'd felt sure it was there, he just wasn't as sure of his ability to help her free it.

Another part of him was thinking about the lonely child inside who'd had to deny who she was for so long that even the woman she'd become didn't recognize herself. He realized that her run at the mirror the day they'd shopped for clothes had been metaphorical.

Then he couldn't think about anything because her hands were in his hair, her lips were at his ear, and he had a handful of her bottom to protect her from going over the side as she leaned into him.

She uttered a small yelp and put a hand to her side where the steering wheel jabbed her.

She looked around, apparently disgusted that she'd wedged him into a corner, her body sprawled over his in a totally delicious but undignified way. He'd have been helpless to defend himself against her had he chosen to, because he had no room to move between the steering wheel and the back of the seat. Actually, the outcome of his little experiment suited him just fine.

She pushed against his chest and sat back in her own seat, straightening her clothes and smoothing her hair. "All right," she said. "Don't look so smug. So you proved half your point."

He drew himself up, still smiling. "Half?"

"You proved she's in there. But—she seldom comes out, so what good does it do you?"

He smiled as he turned the key in the ignition. "She comes out for *me*," he said, emphasizing the important word. "That's all I need to know. We're going for coffee."

LIFE WENT ON for several days in a strange state of anxiety that Athena and David had no choice but to accept.

Athena checked with Holden every day, and every day he told her they were still working through the passenger lists of Northwest flights that had arrived at that time. Several hundred people had picked up baggage at that particular carousel in the two-hour window he'd set up for the investigation.

"It's going to take time," he told her again and again. "All we can do is go through the lists, verify that those people are indeed who they say they are, until we find the one who isn't."

They tried to maintain a regular routine for the boys, who'd both made friends who came home with them from school and ate all Dotty's cookies and played basketball in the driveway until their parents picked them up.

The nightly news still carried Gusty's story, and was now expanded to include the fact that she'd been spotted at the airport.

When Athena was not cooking or cleaning with Dotty or playing basketball with the boys, she brooded over David's kiss.

David was the man she'd dreamed of her entire life,

and now that he had made it clear he wanted a relationship with her even after all she'd done to him, she wanted to run back to D.C.

He didn't love *her*—the courtroom scrapper, the warrior. He loved the woman she simply couldn't be. The woman who'd get hurt if she let her out too often.

She did her best to keep her distance from David, but, despite the big house, the boys seemed to diminish its size. They sprawled in front of the TV in the den, studied in the living room, they had science projects on the dining room table.

David had tried to encourage them to study in their rooms, but they seemed to have a need for company, to hear voices and the sounds of domestic activity. So he relented.

He played the role of father much more than brother, and she found herself admiring the easy way he dealt with them. He tolerated their boyish exuberance and enthusiasm, but if they took one step over the line, he could quell them with a look.

He was in the conservatory when she went in to read and think.

He sat quietly, legs outstretched, eyes unfocused as though he were absorbed in thought. He straightened when he noticed her in the doorway.

"Come in," he invited. "Sit down, relax, do whatever you were going to do." His sober expression lightened as he grinned. "Unless, of course, you'd *like* me to call out the old-fashioned girl."

She gave him a scolding look as she sat across from him in the chair. "No, thank you. I just thought that if I sat someplace quiet, maybe I could somehow connect with Gusty.''

"I hadn't thought of that. Do you two have that twin thing where you...?"

"Experience each other's thoughts?" She shook her head. "No. At least no more than normal sisters would, and then it's more of an empathetic phenomenon than a psychic one. I just thought if I tried to think it all through, something might come to me. What are you thinking about in here all by yourself?"

He hesitated and she heard herself ask gently, "The time the young woman was killed?"

She wasn't sure why she brought it up. The calming atmosphere of the conversatory probably. It would be easier to talk about painful things in this peaceful room and she had a feeling he needed to talk about it. "That wasn't a simple newspaper story, was it? It was part of that other life you lived."

He looked for a moment as though he intended to get to his feet and leave the room. Then he seemed to relax—maybe even to surrender to some force he couldn't fight. "Yes," he said. "It was an assignment in Afghanistan to locate a terrorist."

"Did it go bad?"

He nodded.

"We'd located him and some of his men in a remote camp in the mountains. Farah was a young local woman, our translator and the sister of our guide. She and her brother had worked with us for several weeks, and she and Trevyn got involved. The day we went into the camp, he told her that he didn't want her to come along, but she..." He smiled fondly, reminiscently. "She was a lot like you. Hardheaded. Determined. Without our knowledge, she went ahead to try to distract the men so they wouldn't be aware of us until the very last minute. Meanwhile, her brother, a closet follower of Raisu, had set up an ambush and they got her instead of us."

"How awful." The words were pathetically inadequate, but they were all she had. "I'm sorry."

"Thank you. We all quit when it was over. Bram, because he'd been a soldier then a government agent too long. Trevyn, because he felt murderous and hated that in himself."

"And you?"

She could tell by the look he gave her that she wasn't supposed to ask that question. But she didn't back down.

He relented with a sigh and a shake of his head. "I hated the work. At first it had a sort of swashbuckling charm, you know? You work things behind the scenes and you begin to feel like a hero. Until you realize that in most cases the line between right and wrong and justice and injustice is very thin and often it all comes down to power and the ambitions of some particular politician. I'd wanted out for a while and Farah's death decided me. And even though we didn't get Raisu, we'd flushed him out and another team got him a few days later."

She was sure she wasn't supposed to ask this, either. "Do you still feel responsible for Farah?"

"What are you doing, Athena?" he asked with mild impatience. "What are you trying to make me say?"

She moved to sit beside him on the sofa. He watched her warily.

"I think sometimes there's someone else inside you, too," she said, facing him with her elbow on the back of the sofa and her knees tucked under her. "And you never let him out because he makes you suffer. You're letting him punish you for letting the girl die. That's so unnecessary."

He frowned. "If we're going to quote each other," he said, "how in the hell would *you* know so much about *me?*"

She smiled. "I've watched you operate. You're kind to everyone. You're careful and protective, and I can just imagine that in such work you took every precaution possible. It wasn't your fault."

He leaned back in his corner of the sofa and looked into her eyes. "Why do you want to absolve me?"

She knew, but she couldn't tell him. There were too many other issues in her life that required resolution first.

"I'm not absolving you. You were never guilty."

"But if you're denying that a relationship exists between us, why does it matter to you?"

"Because all those months ago at your party, you told me you wanted to fill this house with children. To have meetings here and noisy parties. My aunt had Christmas parties like that here when we…when Gusty and I were children. I'd like to see that again."

"Really. Well, there's only one way to guarantee that for yourself," he said.

It was too late to evade the obvious answer.

''Do your part to make it happen,'' he added. ''Be the mother of my children.''

She punched his shoulder playfully. ''You don't like me, remember?''

''I never said that,'' he denied. ''I don't like your tactics. You...'' He groaned. ''You are becoming a basic need, like air or water.''

She was jolted by that admission and wanted more than anything to tell him that she needed him every bit as much. But Gusty was missing and accepting love under those circumstances would be such a self-indulgence.

Stammering, unable to explain, she simply excused herself and ran from the room.

Chapter Ten

David crouched down in the concealing bushes, taking a moment to listen, to assess. They'd encountered no one on their way up the mountain and, though Raisu's men would be vigilant, this was mealtime and their attention would be divided.

Trevyn waved a hand at him from the cover of a boulder on the side of the road, and Bram nodded from behind a tree stump.

David waited one more moment. Everyone was tense. They'd been weeks setting this up and success would mean the end of the threat of terrorist activity that hung over American servicemen all over the world. In reprisal for the imprisonment of his captured comrades, Raisu had bombed a tavern frequented by servicemen in Germany, a barracks in Hawaii, a hangar in Aviano, Italy.

David had signaled his readiness to move when they heard the scream and the gunfire that followed.

Even as David experienced a cold rush of dread, thinking that voice sounded familiar, Trevyn bolted toward the sound.

David and Bram followed.

Farah was dead on the narrow road, arms held out in a wide embrace, wearing the camouflage jacket Trevyn had given her during a storm. He'd loved the sight of her small body in it, he'd said, and couldn't take it back.

Her sightless eyes stared at the clear sky.

Trevyn made a sound of animal rage.

Farah's brother Hussein stood in the open several yards away, staring at her body in disbelief, the weapon in his hand still aimed at her.

He'd expected them, David surmised, and been tricked by the jacket.

David had only a moment to assess before the firing started from the other side of the road. He yanked Trevyn down and fired back. Out of the corner of his eye he saw Hussein go down, caught in the crossfire.

Bram appeared beside him, an AKC providing cover fire.

"Get him out of here!" Bram shouted over the noise. "I'm right behind you!"

David pulled Trevyn with him and started down the hill.

But Trevyn yanked himself away, headed back to Farah.

David tried to stop him. "She's gone, Trev!" he said forcefully. "It's just us now and we can't win this one. Help us get out of here!"

"I'm taking her body or I'm not going!" Trevyn shouted, sobbing but perfectly lucid.

David helped him drape the lifeless Farah over his shoulder then, back-to-back with Bram, covered his retreat.

That night David and Bram helped him bury her on the edge of a meadow.

As Trevyn placed her in the grave, David looked down on her to say goodbye. But the eyes looking up at him were Athena's.

He heard himself shout and swear, then he reached for her as Bram would have covered her with dirt.

"No!" he roared at him. "Athena! Athena!"

He heard a small gasp, then became aware of a warm weight on top of him. He opened his eyes to find that he had Athena's wrists in his hands, her body pulled up over his. Brandon and Brady stood behind her, watching with worried frowns.

"Hi," she said softly. "Are you all right?"

He had a death grip on her wrists but she didn't struggle, her eyes urgently trying to read his.

Overcome with relief, David ignored the boys for a moment and pulled Athena closer until he could gather her into his arms.

"You were having a bad dream," she said, touching his face.

"No kidding," he replied roughly.

She tried to ask a question but he shushed her. "Just be still for a minute," he whispered, "and let me enjoy the fact that you're not…that you're alive."

His pulse began to quiet after a moment and he heard the howling wind outside, rain beating against the windows.

He wondered if that was what had planted the notion of gunfire in his subconscious.

"The storm started during the night," Brandon said as he and Brady sat on the other side of the bed. "We don't have any electricity. I wanted to start the generator, but Athena says we better let you do it."

Athena smiled into David's face. "I suppose no power means cereal for breakfast."

David gave her room to move but held his arms loosely around her. "No, it doesn't. We'll have use of the stove and refrigerator, but no lights, I'm afraid."

"It's kinda cool," Brady said. "Sorta like camping. But I wish it coulda happened on a school day instead of a Sunday."

"Dotty says she'll make crepes with strawberries," Brady reported, "'cause Athena liked them so much the other day." He frowned and added, "We were getting dressed and heard you shouting, so Brandon went to get Athena."

David freed Athena and gave each of his brothers a hug. "I'm fine now. Thanks, guys. Why don't you go tell Dotty that I'm up and heading for the generator, then help her set the table."

The boys left the room, pushing and shoving each other into the hallway.

David brought Athena's hands to his lips and kissed her knuckles. "I hope I didn't hurt you."

For the first time since that ugly day, he really understood Trevyn's anguish over Farah. And he understood with empathetic pain for his friend that Trevyn would never wake up and find that her death had been a dream.

"I'm fine," she assured him. "But are you?"

He wasn't sure. The dream had forced him to think again about a time he preferred to forget, and made him aware of just how much Athena now meant to him.

Confounding him further, Athena wrapped him in a quick hug, then leaped off the bed, admonishing him to dress warmly because the house was cold. Then she was gone.

David ran down to the basement to start the generator, then showered and shaved, thanks to a gas water heater. When he arrived downstairs, Brandon and Brady regaled Athena with stories of school and Ferdie's encounter with an angry cat. Dotty had just brought her another crepe.

Athena seemed to be doing her best to be a good audience and an appreciative gourmand, but she looked worried. He understood. Concern for Gusty was never far from their minds.

After breakfast the boys were faced with finding something to do since the power interruption had disabled the television and the computer.

David cut the bottom out of an apple basket. He pulled down a painting that was at about the right height for a basketball hoop, replaced it with the basket, removed the extenders from the dining room table, moved it and the chairs aside, and gave the boys free rein.

"I'd try to find something more creative for them to do," he said to Athena as they began to play, "but their stuff hasn't arrived yet. You can use the sitting room upstairs if you'd like to read. Dotty found all the candles."

"I thought I'd sit in the conservatory. It should be nice and light in there."

"Good idea. But it's chilly, so wear something warm."

He settled there himself with his notes for the rest of his book, trying to drum up sufficient enthusiasm in view of all that had happened, to think about finishing it.

Warmth filled him a few moments later when she returned with a current fashion magazine. She wore her new jeans, a pair of dark blue socks, and the sweatshirt he'd lent her the day she'd rolled Bram's Jeep and he'd picked her up to bring her home.

It made him feel possessive to see her wearing his shirt. She'd cuffed the sleeves back a few times, and it hung on her to mid-thigh, but she had it on over a white blouse, the collar folded over the neckline of the sweatshirt. She looked a little like an ad for an upscale outdoor outfitter.

Her hair was caught back in a simple, straight ponytail that fell to her shoulder blades.

Noticing that he watched her, she took a fistful of the front of the sweatshirt. "Is it all right? I keep forgetting to give it back to you. I bought a sweater with my jeans, but it's a little scratchy."

He forced himself to be casual. She was wary of his attentions, and he didn't want to upset her. "Sure. Consider it yours."

She smiled. "Thank you, David. Is there anything of mine you'd like?" she teased.

The question was ripe for a suggestive answer and though he kept it to himself, she must have read it in his eyes. She whopped him on the head with her magazine, then sat across from him in the chair.

She propped her stockinged feet on the coffee table near his and opened her magazine.

"You considering another line of work?" he asked, finding himself unwilling to go back to his notes. Every day that she spent with him he found it more and more difficult to take his eyes off her. "They don't have clothes for the courtroom in there, do they?"

"I bought it for something to read on the plane," she replied. "I knew I wouldn't be able to think about work, or concentrate on a novel, so I bought something fluffy." She flipped through several pages. "There are a few suits in here."

"What would happen if you walked into the courtroom in a dress?"

"I suppose a serious dress would be all right. High neck, long sleeves, not too fitted."

"Lawyers aren't supposed to look like women?"

She looked at him over the top of the magazine. "No, they're not. You don't want anything to distract the judge or the jury from your questions and your arguments."

That made sense. And it suddenly helped him understand that other side of her. "So that's why the real you is held in check all the time."

She apparently didn't want to discuss that.

He read part of a headline visible on the cover. "There's an article in there about minimalist dressing, according to the cover," he pointed out. "Maybe you'll find courtroom clothes there."

She closed the magazine to consult the cover, and found the appropriate page.

''Well?'' he asked.

She looked up at him again, an eyebrow rippled in consternation, a quirk in the corner of her mouth. ''It's a thong and a bandeau bikini.''

''Now there's a work uniform I could endorse.''

She straightened and raised the rippled eyebrow. ''Maybe you should mind your business and let me read my magazine.''

He pretended hurt feelings and looked to his yellow pad. ''Fine. When Dotty brings the peach tea and the scones, you can just keep reading. When you're finished, I'll let you know how it tasted.''

''Peach tea?''

''Yes.''

''And what kind of scones?''

''Never mind. I'm sure you don't want to be distracted by that while you're studying life-altering lipstick colors and hemline changes.''

''Don't be a chauvinist,'' she scolded. ''There are lots of informative articles in here.''

''Really.''

She cast him a serious glance. '''The Truth about Making Dates on the Internet,''' she read. ''That could be valuable.''

''Could be.''

'''How to Seduce Your Man into Giving You What You Want.'''

''Would you do that?'' he asked.

''It would depend on what I wanted and how badly I wanted it,'' she said. Then she made a face and said wryly, ''No, I wouldn't. I'm not much of a game-player. I'd probably just tell him what I wanted and make the best case possible for why I should have it."

He liked her answer. "That's interesting."

"Why? Would you be vulnerable to a seduction?"

"Sure I would," he replied. "But if you wanted something and *I* was your man, all you'd have to do is ask me."

He went back to his notes and let that sink in.

"Then," she asked, "if I ask you to share the peach tea and scones with me when they come, you will?"

"Sure." He smiled at her.

She went back to her magazine, he waited a moment then asked, "You realize that means you're admitting I'm your man?"

She did not lower the magazine. "Read your notes, David," she replied.

FOR THE FIRST TIME in a week, Athena felt herself relax. She hadn't forgotten Gusty and Lex, and she wasn't ignoring their disappearances, but there was something about the laughter of the boys in the other room and the quiet presence of David across from her in the conservatory that allowed her—for this small space of time—to just be.

And she couldn't forget the pained and desperate sound of David's voice as he shouted her name just before he awoke. She guessed he dreamed about that last mission where the woman Trevyn loved had died. Had his subconscious somehow replaced *her* with the woman? He'd held her as though afraid of letting her go. She was unwilling to look too closely at what that meant.

As rain beat at the windows and the wind whipped up the surf and shook the bushes and trees, they were safe in their Cliffside cocoon—and that was sufficient blessing for the moment.

Soon the aroma of something baking permeated the downstairs, and Dotty arrived with tea and scones. The boys joined them in the conservatory and Ferdie moved from one person to another mooching bites.

Brandon frowned over the taste of the tea.

David offered him the sugar bowl. "Here. This helps."

Several spoons seemed to make his tea more palatable and he sat beside Athena's chair, Ferdie resting his head on his knee.

Brady sat with David on the sofa, eating hungrily. "Wouldn't it be cool," he asked, "if we went straight from this storm into snow so we wouldn't have to go back to school?"

"Then you wouldn't know anything when you grew up," Brandon said, "and you couldn't get a job."

"I'd stay here with David." Brady seemed unconcerned by that prediction. "He'd take care of me, wouldn't ya?"

"Sure, I would," David replied. "But the day you turn eighteen, I'm charging you rent."

Brady frowned. "But I'll be going to college. I won't be able to pay rent."

"You won't be able to go to college if you don't go to school."

Brady made a face at him, a good-natured grin behind it. "You set me up."

"I did, but that's really the way it works."

Brady put his empty plate on the coffee table and leaned back contentedly. "I don't care. I was just teasing about school. I like it, I just don't like having to do homework." He turned to David with a lazy smile. "But I like it here so much, I'll do it anyway."

"Are we gonna get an allowance?" Brandon asked.

David shook his head. "I'm just going to use you as slaves."

Brandon looked up at Athena, a twinkle in his eye telling her he knew he was being teased. "Would you let him do that?" he asked.

"I don't have anything to say about it." She ruffled Brandon's hair. "Sorry."

"But injustice is everyone's business," he said, playfully theatrical.

She laughed, meeting the amusement in David's eyes. "He's got us there."

"You live here," Brady said. "And you're a grown-up. You get a vote, don't you?"

"I don't *live* here," she corrected, "I'm just a houseguest."

The boy looked suddenly stricken and turned to David. "Does that mean she's gonna leave?"

"She has to find her sister first," David placated.

"*Then* she's gonna leave?" Brady was *not* placated.

David met her uncertain expression across the

small space and had no difficulty tossing the responsibility back to her. "That's pretty much her call."

"I think she should just stay," Brady said.

"Me, too," Brandon agreed, then winked at her. "Particularly if she can get us an allowance."

"I'm open to arguments," David said, then met her eyes and added significantly, "or the technique we discussed earlier. You remember? The article in the magazine about how to get what you want from a man."

He was suggesting she try seduction. As though her life wasn't already too complicated.

ATHENA HAD TO ADMIT to herself that that possibility had considerable appeal. She'd never met a man who appreciated her skills and abilities, and still made her feel as though he would stand with his dying breath between her and whatever threatened her.

It was what every woman dreamed of, she thought with a private smile. A man who would consider a woman his equal, but still be willing to protect her from all the things that frightened her.

But what did she have to offer him? she wondered. She was dissatisfied with her job, confused about herself, and apparently no one in her life considered her worthy of their confidences.

She smiled from one boy to the other. "How about if I just give each of you ten bucks instead of trying to get you an allowance?"

She expected instant acceptance of her offer. She was surprised when even Brady frowned. "That

won't work. What'll we do next week? No. You have
to talk David into it.''

Brandon rose up on his knees, dislodging Ferdie,
and folded his arms on the arms of her chair. ''Lawyers sometimes get hired as…um…arbor—something?'' He turned to David.

''Arbitrators,'' David provided, his eyes still
amused. She wasn't going to get out of this.

''That's it!'' Brandon's blue eyes were lively with
what he seemed to feel sure was a plan.

Athena was momentarily distracted by how much
the boy had changed in one short week. David also
stood between him and what would harm him and it
was clear he'd blossomed under that knowledge.

''Can you do it?'' he asked her. ''If we hire you
as our arbitrator? Can you get us an allowance? And
stay?''

''I'll see what I can do.''

The boys went back to their basketball game, and
David put his notes aside and folded his arms expec-
tantly.

''Relax,'' she said. ''I have to work on my strategy.
But why don't you just give them an allowance?''

''I was going to,'' he said, and grinned, ''but Brandon's idea has such promise, I figured I'd go with it.''

''You just told me,'' she reminded him judiciously,
''that if you were my man, I'd only have to ask you
for what I wanted.''

''That's true,'' he conceded. ''But you're asking
me for what *they* want. Not the same thing at all.''

She smiled blandly at him. ''*You* should be a lawyer.''

THE STORM QUIETED in the middle of the afternoon and power was restored a short time later.

The boys groaned as they took down the apple basket and reassembled the dining room in preparation for dinner.

"Dining room basketball was fun!" Brady said, pushing chairs up to the table. "Now I s'pose we have to go back to school tomorrow."

"Yeah." Brandon replaced a pot of flowers in the middle of the table. "But we have TV tonight."

"Oh, yeah!" That brought Brady out of his depression and he was heard laughing as he and Brandon went to the den.

"Telephone call for Brandon," Dotty said, peering out of the kitchen. She added worriedly to David, "I think it's your mother."

David went into the kitchen and took the phone, Athena trailing.

"Yes?" he asked.

"David." Jordana sounded surprised. "I wanted to speak to Brandon."

"He's getting ready for dinner," David said calmly, though he suspected some kind of intrigue at work here. "Can I give him a message?"

She was silent for a moment, then she replied a little aggressively, "Tell him we've changed our minds and Darby's coming for him and Brady tomorrow."

David had been in enough battles of one kind or another to easily recognize another one. The objective was Brandon's trust fund, and the weapons were Brandon and Brady.

It was time to take a stand.

"They're staying with me," he said. "Tell Darby not to bother to come. I'm getting a lawyer and filing for custody."

There was surprised sputtering and stammering on the other end of the line. "They are *my* children!"

"You don't have children, Jordana, you have kids you use to your advantage, to manipulate their fathers with, or, in Darby's case, to attract prospective husbands with the promises of wealth. What's happened? Is your money running out and you need Brandon's trust fund?"

"How dare you?"

"Is it?"

"We have responsibilities!" she said with injured dignity. "And the money would help us—"

"Meet Darby's gambling debts?" he asked. "Or is the day trading not going well?"

There was a moment of shocked silence. "David, it's none of your business," she said finally.

"They're staying here."

"All right," she said after a moment. "If it's a fight you want, we'll give you one. But Darby will be there to pick up the boys tomorrow, and if you stand in his way, we'll bring in the police. The law is *not* on your side, David."

"We'll see. Goodbye, Jordana."

He hung up the phone, his insides trembling with anger. Unfortunately, she was right, David thought. Jordana was their mother and it would be difficult to prove by her palatial surroundings that the boys were neglected.

Still, Darby was a new, darker element in the boys' lives and David wasn't letting them go.

Dotty, who'd overheard his end of the conversation, and probably deduced the rest, asked worriedly, "What are you going to do?"

"I'm going to hire an attorney," he said firmly.

"You have one," Athena said. "And for you, I'll keep the billable hours way down." Then she asked more seriously. "What do you need?"

He repeated his conversation with Jordana. "I need the impossible."

"Nothing's impossible. What?"

"I need a way to be able to keep them even though she's their mother. The law's on her side. I could take her to court, but I don't think the emotional neglect and the disregard for their feelings—like sending Ferdie to the pound—would stand up in court. Anyway, Darby's supposed to be coming for them tomorrow, and I told her I wasn't letting him have them."

"You think she just wants them back because of Brandon's inheritance?"

"I'm sure of it. According to the boys, Darby's a gambler. And Brandon says he's been day-trading. You can lose a fortune in no time that way."

She nodded. "Okay. We've got one day to work on it. What time's dinner, Dotty?"

"Twenty minutes," the housekeeper returned.

"Okay. I have a couple of phone calls to make." She patted his shoulder. "Don't worry. I'm going to do this for you."

"How?"

"Just trust me."

Chapter Eleven

Athena realized that might be a foolish request considering the things she'd done to him in the past. "Can you do that?" she asked.

He caught her arm, pulled her to him and kissed her soundly. "I can do that. Thank you for wanting to help."

"They mean a lot to me, too." She forced an even tone of voice, though the kiss left her just a little shaken. She felt warm and soft and maternal toward the boys. And decidedly sexual about David.

It was that other woman his kisses brought out, she thought.

She ran upstairs, called Patrick, told him the story and gave him her instructions. Then she went down to dinner.

DOTTY WAS SERVING dessert when the telephone rang again. She turned back toward the kitchen, but David stopped her on the chance that it was Jordana again.

"I'll get it," he said.

"Mr. Hartford, this is Parker Johns," a polite voice said.

The name sounded vaguely familiar. Jordana's attorney, perhaps? "Yes?"

"From the Wallace, White and Whitcomb Agency?" the voice prompted.

Wallace, White and...? And then it struck him like a frying pan to the head. The literary agent to whom he'd sent his book!

"Is this a bad time?" Johns asked. "I know it's a little late for a business call, but I just finished your proposal for *Jake's Journal* and frankly, I'm excited. I think I can sell this for you."

David stared at the phone, speechless. *You should be cool,* he told himself. *This is no different than a covert government operation with a lot at stake.*

But he remembered the lonely hours at the computer, the anguish over character development that required reliving much of what he'd personally been through, the ripping out of plot turns to try something different, hopefully better, then reading it over and over for pacing and flow.

"You're kidding!" he finally said, aware that his remark was less than cool.

Johns laughed. "Not at all. It's a firm, hard-hitting story with a very strong main character. I'd like to see what you've done with the rest of it. Can you over-night it to me?"

David thought worriedly about Jordana's push to get the boys back and the last chapter of the book he just couldn't quite put together.

"I have some pressing family issues at the moment," he said, fully expecting the opportunity to fall apart on him. "And the last chapter isn't finished."

"Can you send what you've got?" Johns persisted. "First thing in the morning?"

"Yes," he replied. "Sure."

"Okay. Take down this number. When you're finished with that last chapter, I want you to fax it to me, all right?"

"All right."

"The sooner the better."

"I understand."

"I'll be in touch after I've read the rest. And good luck with the family issue."

David went back to the table in a state of mild shock.

He smiled into Dotty's and Athena's concerned expressions.

"I have an agent," he said, toasting them with his coffee cup, "interested in representing my book."

Athena applauded and Dotty squealed. The boys looked puzzled.

"What does that mean?" Brandon asked.

"An agent is someone who'll take my book around to various publishers," he explained, "and try to sell it for me."

"I thought it wasn't finished yet," Brady said.

"It isn't. But he likes what he's seen so far and wants me to send him as much as I have finished."

"That's great." Brandon beamed and returned David's toast with his glass of milk. "Congratulations." He sobered for a moment. "That doesn't mean we have to leave, does it?"

"No," David replied firmly. "But it might mean you'll have to be quieter while I'm working."

"We can do that," Brandon said. He added, with an elbow jab at Brady, "We may have to gag him, but we can do that."

WHEN THEY'D FINISHED EATING, the boys went into the living room to finish their homework, unaware of the intrigue underway on their behalf. Athena couldn't bear the thought of their being forced to go back to their mother. She tried to help Dotty clean up, but she shooed her away.

"I'm sure you have things to do," she said. "Go on. I'll finish up here then I'm off to my room for a Doris Day movie marathon."

"I love Doris Day!" Athena carried a stack of plates to the sink.

"Well, one day I'll invite you to join me. But, for now, go sit down. I'll have fresh coffee brewed in a minute."

Athena called Lex, hoping against hope that she would answer. But all she heard was the same bilingual message.

It was odd, she thought as she listened to the once familiar voice, how disconnected she felt from her old life.

Her family had been dispersed for much of her adult life, but—except for her grinding concern for her sisters—she felt as though her family was here.

It had been just a little more than a week, but when she wasn't thinking of Gusty or Lex, she was all wrapped up in what was happening at Cliffside.

That didn't sound like a cool, detached woman, did it? she asked herself. She wondered how she could measure whether or not she had changed, and if so, how much. But she could think of no way to assess that.

She called good-night to the boys, then went downstairs to make sure all the candles they'd used during the power outage had been snuffed.

She met David, standing alone in the dim glow of one kitchen light and staring into a cup of coffee.

"What is it?" she asked, leaning against the counter beside him.

"I was thinking," he said moodily, "that life isn't that much different than espionage."

She raised an eyebrow at that, a little worried about his quiet mood considering the wonderful news about his book. "Really."

He nodded, looking toward the darkness beyond the window. "There's a lot less blood and guts, of course, but there's also a lot of mystery involved, you seldom know where you stand, it seems you have to fight someone for everything you want, and in the end, if you emerge with your sanity and your skin, you're doing well."

She found herself nudging her way into his arms, wrapping hers around his waist and leaning into him. "I'm going to get your brothers for you," she said firmly.

She felt him pull her closer, rub gently up and down her arm. "How? I've been thinking about it, trying to come up with a plan that doesn't involve dragging the kids into court and making them talk about what they don't have in their lives—and I can't."

She raised her head to kiss his cheek. "That's because you're not the lawyer. I am. I told you to leave it to me. You just worry about getting the rest of the manuscript off to your agent and finish the last chapter."

He rubbed his forehead wearily. "I can mail off what I've got, but I can't even think about the rest of it until I know—"

"You promised to trust me," she reminded him. "You're not weaseling on me, are you?"

He hugged her to him. "Of course not."

Was this the proof she was looking for, she wondered? The willingness to pull out of her own gummy problems to help him relieve his? The concern with the grim look on his face and the need to give him something to smile about? The contentment that came from the simple touch of his arm across her shoulders?

"And what are you going to do?" he challenged, kissing the top of her head.

"I never discuss my strategy." She tipped her head back to look into his eyes. The grimness hadn't been banished, but it had receded and there was a smile on his lips.

Suddenly something else defined this moment for her. The urgent desire to communicate what she felt for him, confusion and uncertainties and all.

She stood on tiptoe, wrapped her arms around his neck and kissed him.

DAVID WONDERED if he'd put too much brandy in his coffee. She'd never initiated physical contact. She hadn't drawn away from it over the past few days, but she'd never touched him first.

Now her body slid sinuously against his as she rose on tiptoe, and there was a languorous desire in her eyes as she looked into his before claiming his mouth.

A woman taking control was new for him. His back-alley combat experience usually took charge before a woman had a chance to make a move.

Was this what real love was all about? he wondered. The willingness to surrender to someone else's control, however temporarily?

"When we find Gusty," she whispered, her breath on his cheek, "I'm handcuffing her to a kitchen chair and I'm not letting her out of my sight."

He kissed the tip of her nose. "Until that happens," he replied softly, "you can handcuff me to anything you want. To you would be preferable, but I'm open to suggestions."

She laughed lightly, leaning her forehead against his chin. "In the absence of handcuffs, what if I just use my magnetic personality to hold you?" she teased in a whisper.

"That would work," he replied softly.

She laced her fingers in his as they leaned into each other. "I'd like very much," she said, "to make love with you right now. Would you...?"

That was the easiest decision he'd ever made. He lifted her into his arms in reply, and carried her upstairs to his room. It was dark and cool and the quiet shadows were so inviting that he didn't bother with a light.

He put her down at the foot of the bed and felt her

hands at the hem of his sweater. He reached for hers and they undressed each other in easy, unhurried movements, like peeling away layers of shadow until an alabaster vision appeared before him, diffused by the darkness.

He drew her to him and felt her little sigh of pleasure as they stood body to body, her softness melding into him, the tips of her breasts beading against his ribs.

Her hands went to his back and he felt them explore his shoulders, roam down his spinal column to the small of his back. He waited for her hands to glide lower, but she raised them instead and tightened her grip around his waist.

"I love you," she said against his collarbone. "I'm shocked, amazed, confounded. This shouldn't happen to two people in ten days' time, should it?"

"I don't think that matters," he said. He swept a hand down her spine, then shaped her hip in it and stroked the curve with his thumb. "It happened. I love you, too. I have since that night on the stairs at the party."

He tossed the blankets back and lifted her into the middle of the bed, then climbed in beside her and drew the covers over them.

ATHENA WAS ALREADY ATREMBLE and he had yet to touch her again. So she reached for him, wrapping her arms around his neck and clinging as emotions spiraled out of her—fear, worry, hope, passion. She'd done her best to maintain a hopeful attitude and at least an outward demeanor of self-control.

But there were times when she'd felt pretty desperate inside.

What was bringing this on? she wondered as her body shuddered. They were making love. She felt secure in him and he in her.

And then as he lay on his back to support her embrace, she realized what it was. He was all long, strong muscle under her, steely arms around her, confidence in his touch and in his voice.

His hands explored her, then stopped when he felt her trembling against him.

"Are you all right?" he asked.

"I think so," she said, still holding him. "I think this is just some emotional upheaval, or something. I'll be fine. I know this isn't the time for—"

"It's time for sharing," he said, kissing her shoulder, "concerns as well as celebrations. Do you need to talk?"

She thought about that a moment but decided that wasn't the communication she needed.

"Thank you, but I don't. Unless you'd like to hear me tell you again that I love you."

He kissed her in response and in a moment she was able to stop thinking and simply feel. His fingertips on her skin, his lips on her breast, the suede of his skin under her hands.

She rained kisses on his chest while he explored every inch of her until he finally held her astride his waist and entered her in a swift and sure move that brought them together and suddenly made sense of the universe.

This was it, she thought, as they moved together, fingers locked. Destiny. Harmony. Love.

DAVID FELT SUDDENLY and permanently transformed. It wasn't a vast difference that changed the scope of his world, but the small, subtle shift of a piece of life's puzzle that hadn't fit before but did now—and finally made him whole.

Afterward, they lay together, arms and legs entangled, and he noticed that she'd stopped trembling.

"Feel better?" he asked.

"I feel," she said, running a lazy foot along his shin, "as though we were made just for each other to hold on to. But I suppose we'll have to let go eventually. You know, to go to work, or go shopping."

He laughed. "Twins of another sort, huh?"

ATHENA FELT A SUDDEN JOLT of alarm. She'd intended to tell him the truth about being a triplet instead of a twin earlier tonight. But she'd looked into his eyes and seen love there and everything else had been swept from her brain.

"What?" he asked gently, brushing the hair from her face.

As though on cue from her scattered wits, her stomach growled.

"Ah," he said. "That's right. You're a midnight fridge raider. You stay here, and I'll get some leftovers and a bottle of wine."

A reprieve! Time to think about how best to approach an explanation! "That sounds wonderful," she said.

He gave her one quick kiss, pulled on jeans and a T-shirt and left the room.

She put both hands to her eyes and wondered how she could keep making things worse.

Chapter Twelve

David uncorked a bottle of Sokol Blosser white zinfandel and was slicing leftover pot roast when the phone rang. He glanced at the clock in surprise. It was well after ten o'clock.

He reached for the wall phone. "Hello?"

"Davey!" David barely recognized Henry Wren's voice in the cacophonic disturbance going on in the background on his end of the line. There were screams, shouts, loud mechanical sounds.

"Henry?" David asked. "Where are you? What's going on?"

"We've got her!" Henry said. That was followed by an odd blunt sound, Henry's rich oath, then the muffled: "Will you please get control of her before we're all killed? What in the hell do I pay you for, anyway!"

David felt adrenaline race through his body. They'd found Gusty!

"Henry? Where are you?"

"In a chopper headed your way," he replied, shouting above the background noise. "Davey, I hope you've got a rubber room for this young lady. Did her sister say she was sweet? If so, the amnesia's caused some sort of psychotic episode, or something.''

There was crashing and more shouting in the background.

''What's your ETA?'' David asked.

''Ten minutes,'' Henry replied. ''You might alert the Coast Guard in case we end up in the drink!''

''Get her here, Henry,'' David said. ''I'll put lights on for you.''

David hung up the phone then ran to put on all the outside lights. He'd have alerted Athena first, but didn't want Henry's chopper to arrive in the dark.

Then he ran out to the garage, opened all the doors and put on the headlights on all three vehicles.

When he ran back into the house, Athena was half-way down the stairs in his long robe, her hair a rumpled mass around her. ''Is something wrong?'' she asked worriedly. ''I heard you go outside.''

''Henry found her,'' he said, leaving the front door open and beckoning her to join him.

''Who's Henry?'' she asked, coming toward him in her bare feet.

''The friend I asked to look for Gusty. He found her.''

She gaped at him in disbelief, her mouth opening to form words but apparently unable.

''He expected to be here in ten—'' He stopped at the distant sound of rotors. ''There he is! Stay in here and I'll…''

She was already out the door and running toward

the middle of the lawn in her bare feet. He followed, caught her arm and pulled her back to the doorway, wrapping both arms around her to keep here there.

''He needs room to put down!'' he said, over the now deafening sound.

Then the chopper was overhead, a blinding light creating a broad circle in the middle of the lawn. The helicopter hovered for a moment, then slowly came down. David shielded Athena's face with his own as debris blew around them.

Athena tried to run toward it when it touched down, but David held on to her until the rotors finally stopped. Then she was gone like a shot.

He followed slowly as she ran, grateful that all of this was going to end happily after all.

The bay door on the side slid open and a young man in jeans and a sweatshirt leaped down.

''Where is she?'' Athena demanded, ignoring the man's attempt to guide her out of the way and leaning into the dimly lit interior.

Remembering what Henry had said about Gusty having some kind of psychotic problem, David hurried forward and drew Athena back out of the way.

He was just in time to avoid a pair of legs, tied together at the ankles, as they kicked their way out of the helicopter.

The young man caught the feet, Henry appearing in the open doorway, holding on to the woman's arms. She was wearing a camouflage coat many sizes too large for her. Dark red hair streamed across her face and hung down behind her as Henry pitched her forward and the young man swept her into his arms. Her hands had been tied and she'd been gagged. She still struggled valiantly.

"My God!" Athena shrieked, hurrying after the young man as he strode determinedly toward the house. "Put her down!"

"Can't ma'am. Not until we're inside."

Henry tossed out a small suitcase, then a large leather satchel, and leaped down after them.

"We'll just be a couple of minutes," he said to the pilot.

"I'll be here," the pilot's voice replied, "thanking God that she didn't pitch us into the sea."

David slung the bags over his shoulder and led Henry toward the house. "You're still the best!" he said gratefully. "I owe you big, Henry."

"You bet you do," Henry said. "She just about killed the three of us. For a woman who doesn't know who she is, she sure as hell knows what she wants. And she did not want to come with us."

"Did you explain that you were taking her to her sister?"

He nodded. "That was when she went ballistic on us."

"She probably doesn't remember she has a sister."

"Maybe. And you were wrong about some of the details you gave me."

"What do you mean?"

"Check the wallet in her purse," he said as they reached the front door. "Let's talk inside. And you owe me a good stiff drink and combat pay for this."

ATHENA KNEW WHAT WAS WRONG before the young man put her sister on her feet in the middle of the living room.

Athena held her arm to steady her as he untied her ankles, then caught her arm to hold her in place as she kicked at him, muffled threats coming from behind the bandanna tied around her mouth. He untied her hands and moved away nimbly.

Wide-eyed recognition registered in the bright blue gaze above the bandanna for the first time since she'd been unceremoniously unloaded with her hair over her face, then carried to the house.

Athena yanked down the gag and pulled off the coat.

"Athena!" her sister gasped, spitting cotton fuzz. "What is going on? And where..." She looked around herself in surprise, rubbing her now unshackled wrists. "Cliffside? We're at Cliffside?"

Athena led her to a chair, but not before her sister aimed a punch at the man who'd carried her in. He danced out of her way.

"Yes, we are," Athena replied. "Are you all right?"

"Am I all right? All right! I'm followed by two men into the rental car lot at the Portland airport, told to come with them because they're going to take me to my sister, and when I resist because what woman in her right mind would swallow that story from two guys who look like something out of *The Dirty Dozen!* They grab me, put me on a helicopter, then tie my hands and feet when I put up a struggle! No, I'm not all right! I'm mad as hell and I want to know right this minute what's going on!" Her eyes focused suddenly on Athena's robe and she asked with a frown, "What are you doing here? Is Gusty here?"

Athena looked toward the door, hoping she'd been fortunate enough that David hadn't heard that question.

But he stood in the middle of the living room, an open wallet in his hand, thunder in his expression.

"*Alexis* Ames?" he asked Athena, apparently having just read Lex's driver's license.

"Yes," she said, a sense of impending doom settling into the pit of her stomach. "Lexie, this is David Hartford, our...host. David, this is my second sister, Alexis." She didn't know if she had to clarify that or not, but there was a certain relief in finally saying it. "I'm a triplet, not a twin."

There was a moment's stunned silence, then she heard Henry say sharply, "What?"

"Wow!" said a high-pitched voice from the stairway.

Athena turned around to see Brandon and Brady standing at the bottom of the stairs, Brandon holding an interested Ferdie by the collar.

"There's *another* one!" Brady said.

Dotty ran in from the back of the house, belting her robe, and stopped to stare in amazement at the large number of people in the living room.

"Shall I make coffee?" she asked into the silence.

David stared at Athena one more moment, anger emanating from every pore, then he nodded at Dotty, pointed Henry and his partner to the sofa and the boys to the kitchen.

Athena noticed that everyone hurried to comply, David's expression an ominous thing.

"You mean I got the wrong woman?" Henry asked as David crossed the room to Alexis. "But she looks…"

"It's all right," David assured him quickly. "You had incomplete information. My fault." As he accepted the blame, he glanced at Athena, his eyes telling her they'd settle up on that score later.

He sat on the hassock in front of Alexis's chair. "I apologize for what happened tonight," he said. "Henry's a friend of mine, and I'd asked him to try to find Gusty. I didn't realize there was a third look-alike."

"We had to tie her up," Henry said defensively. "She was hitting us and kicking at the pilot. Lance, here—" he indicated his partner "—is going to be a soprano for a couple of days. We almost crashed into the ocean."

"And we thought it was for her own good," Lance added. "You said she had amnesia."

David nodded his understanding. "I accept full responsibility." To Alexis, he added, "I can't tell you how sorry I am."

Alexis met his eyes with a steady stare, then sighed and seemed to relent. "This was my destination, though I'd expected to arrive by rental car rather than by helicopter."

"Where have you been?" Athena demanded, ignoring David's glare her way at the interruption. "I've been trying to call you for days!"

"I went to the French countryside," Lex replied,

still rubbing her wrists, "trying to kick-start some creative spark. On my way home I stopped to have dinner at the American Club in Paris and saw Gusty on the news! I tried to call your office, but they said you'd come to Cliffside."

"Why didn't you call my cell phone?"

"I didn't have the number."

"I left it on your answering machine."

"But I didn't even go home. I had a bag with me, so I booked a flight right then and there." She gave Henry and Lance a brief, disparaging glance. "These two picked me up when I flew into Portland."

"I was monitoring calls to Athena's office and her condo in Boston," Henry explained, "on the chance that her sister did remember something and called her. Fortunately, Alexis used a phone card to make that call, so when I saw that her name was Ames, I thought we had her. I figured you were just mistaken about the first name—Alexis, Augusta. I tracked her reservation to fly to Portland, and when I saw she wasn't pregnant, I thought she had the baby while she was missing."

"What do you do, anyway?" Alexis asked Henry. "And is it legal?"

Henry smiled. "Depends on who you ask. So, David, am I still looking, or am I fired?"

"You're still looking," David replied, and headed for the kitchen. "I'll get you that drink."

Henry stood. "Thanks, but I've got to get the copter back."

"Then hold on a minute," David called over his

shoulder, "and I'll get you some coffee in a thermos. Your pilot could probably use some caffeine."

Several minutes later David walked Henry and Lance out to the helicopter, Henry carrying the promised thermos and a bag of cookies Dotty had provided.

Athena sat opposite Alexis, delighted beyond measure that at least one of her sisters was safe in front of her. Another part of her was filled with regret that she'd lied to David about Alexis and that he'd found out about it this way.

"What *are* you doing here?" Alexis asked, leaning toward her.

Athena noticed that she looked exhausted. It was a long flight to the West Coast from Europe, and making the last leg of it tied up in a helicopter could not have been pleasant.

"I saw Gusty on the news, too, and went to Astoria to pick her up at the hospital. David had also come for the same reason. Only she was already gone. So we decided to team up and try to find her."

"I don't get it. Why did *he* go to the hospital?"

"Because he thought he was the father of her baby."

"What? Why would he...?" Alexis began to ask, then stopped, her eyes widening as the obvious occurred to her. "You mean...the night of the costume party?"

Athena nodded.

"They made love?"

"No. He was with me that night. He just thought it was her."

Alexis looked puzzled, then dubious. "*You* made love with him the night of the party?"

"No! He just thought…" Athena stopped as Dotty placed on the coffee table a tea tray and a plate of cookies. When the housekeeper disappeared again, she repeated, "He just thought we did. He'd had antihistamines and too much champagne and passed out."

Alexis leaned back in her chair and closed her eyes. "Maybe I'm just too tired, but I'm really confused."

"We all are," David said, pushing the outside door closed. He locked it and came to look down on them. "Alexis, you're welcome to stay, of course, until we find Gusty."

"Thank you, David." She glanced in the direction of the kitchen. "I didn't realize you had children. I thought you lived here on your own with a couple of friends in the rentals."

"The boys are my brothers," David replied. "My life's undergone a fairly dramatic change in the past week and a half. When you two are finished catching up," he said with an unreadable glance in Athena's direction, "I'd like to talk to you."

"Sure." Athena nodded, knowing there was no escape.

When he left them alone, Athena told Lex everything she knew about Gusty's disappearance, from the accident that led to the photo that made the news and her amnesia, to the boys thinking they'd spotted her at the airport and the investigation under way of the passenger lists for Northwest flights that had arrived near the time of the boys' plane.

"I've been checking with Officer Holden daily," Athena said, "but so far, everyone checks out."

"And the boys said she was with a scary-looking guy?" Lex asked worriedly.

Athena nodded. "We're hoping they misinterpreted his expression. You know how kids are. If an adult doesn't smile at them, they're sure he's mean."

Lex nodded halfheartedly. "I didn't know Gusty was pregnant. Did you?"

"No." Athena tugged at the lapels of the robe she'd borrowed. "And I have no idea what she was doing in Oregon, either. Do you remember anything about the Musketeer you were with the night of the party?"

Lex looked surprised by the question. "Yeah. Mostly what I told you. That he seemed too sweet to have done anything like hurt Aunt Sadie or steal from her."

"But I mean anything that would help us decide which of David's friends you spent that time with."

She thought back. "He was cute. I mean in manner, since I couldn't see his face. He was funny. Gentlemanly in a bossy sort of way."

Athena nodded impatiently. "But anything physical? Think, Lex. I waited for you for half an hour. You had to have noticed something."

"I didn't," she insisted. "We were masked, remember, and you said to try to keep our identities secret, so when I wouldn't tell him who I was, he said he wouldn't tell me. That way neither of us would feel inhibited."

Athena groaned.

"Why?" Lex demanded. "You didn't know who you'd been with, either. You told me that night that you didn't. None of us did. Although..."

"Although, what?" Athena asked eagerly.

"Although...he saw me before I left."

"What do you mean?"

"We were dancing and I told him I had to leave. He lifted my mask and he kissed me." Her eyes lost focus and she smiled a little sadly. Then she straightened and sighed. "I ran out. I heard him try to follow, but I lost him in the darkness."

Athena shook her head. "Great. I thought you'd have some clue."

"Why is that so important?"

"Because," Athena replied, "whoever *wasn't* with you, could be the father of Gusty's baby."

"Oh." Lex leaned back against the cushions. "Next time you get an idea for the three of us to crash a masked ball, I'm hitting you with a blunt object."

She sat up again suddenly. "Did you find out why Aunt Sadie left David the house?"

Athena smiled ruefully. "Are you ready for this?"

Alexis winced. "After today, I should be ready for anything. What?"

"They were spies together," Athena explained. "Knowing Sadie, should we really be surprised? Apparently David saved her life on a job in Africa, so she left him the house."

Alexis stared at her as she absorbed that information. "Our aunt was a spy," she said flatly. "And David..."

"And his friends."

"Good Lord."

Knowing that she'd stalled as long as she could, Athena stood. "Why don't you have another cup of tea. I saw Dotty go upstairs with fresh linens, so your room should be ready in a few minutes. I have to talk to David."

Lex frowned. "Why did David think we were twins?"

"Because," Athena replied, "the policeman at the hospital thought I was Gusty's twin, and I just let him believe it. I didn't know what was going on, what David was doing there or why Gusty was missing, and I thought another sister who looked just like us that no one knew about might come in handy."

Alexis groaned. "But that kind of thing always got us in trouble as kids."

"Yeah." Athena backed toward the kitchen. "I guess there's comfort in the fact that some things never change."

Chapter Thirteen

David had fixed the boys a cup of hot cocoa and a plate of cookies, fed a cookie to Ferdie, then sent them all up to bed again by the back stairs when Athena walked into the kitchen.

He had promised himself that he wouldn't shout at her. It was his fault that he'd believed anything she'd told him. Hadn't she lied to him about absolutely everything since the night of the party when she'd beguiled him on the stairs?

He sat at the small table with a cup of coffee and she came to sit opposite him. She looked apologetic—and exhausted.

"At the risk of splitting hairs," she said, "Officer Holden told you I was a twin, I didn't."

"And someone gagged you," he suggested conversationally, "and prevented you from correcting him? Or later explaining to me?"

He'd promised himself not to shout. He hadn't promised anything about not being angry.

She acknowledged that absurdity with a roll of her eyes. "No, but at that time I still thought you might have hurt or somehow coerced my aunt into leaving you Cliffside and I thought it might help to have Lex outside the situation, possibly able to help me.''

He nodded. ''Ah. And you still thought that tonight when you made love with me? Because I don't ever remember you clarifying that.''

She nodded guiltily. ''I meant to.''

''But you didn't.''

''I know, but everything got so entangled, and I couldn't reach Lex to tell her about Gusty, and then it got to where I wasn't even sure who was missing.'' She was beginning to sound a little desperate, but he refused to let himself sympathize. ''And then it was like I just...sort of...forgot I hadn't told you. I remembered tonight, and came into the kitchen to tell you when the house was finally quiet, but you looked so worried, and I wanted to make you feel better.''

''And you forgot again.''

''Yes.''

''Have you stopped to count how many things you've lied to me about?''

She sighed defeatedly. ''No, I haven't.''

''I think it'd require a calculator.''

''David,'' she said plaintively.

''So I can only conclude,'' he went on, ''that everything you've told me is a lie. Isn't that courtroom technique? If the witness has lied about anything, you can dismiss his entire testimony?''

She looked him in the eye, her expression pugnacious. ''I didn't lie about loving you. Did tonight feel like a lie? Certainly a man who has learned to read people and situations like you have would know the difference!''

"A large part of my life until recently," he replied, "was all about tricks and lies and traitorous behavior. I don't need that in my personal life."

She raised both hands helplessly, her face pale, her eyes miserable. "Then you don't have to worry about it anymore. Good night."

All right, he told himself, he'd carried that too far. She'd been wrong and he was right, but she'd lied to him because she thought he was a threat to her family, then to enlist his help in finding her sister.

So, maybe she had forgotten about the twin-triplet detail. Things had been a little chaotic around here.

He carried his cup to the sink, rinsed it out, then put it in the dishwasher. Dotty returned with the empty tray and said good-night.

"We can talk about double-overtime in the morning," she said with a grin.

He went into the living room, expecting to find Athena with her sister, but the room was empty, except for the teapot and a half-empty cup. He banked the fire.

Upstairs he heard soft music coming from one of the previously empty rooms and guessed Alexis was settling in for the night.

Athena's door was closed. He hesitated in front of it, then decided against disturbing her. He wasn't sure what to say, anyway. She seemed to find it impossible to be honest with him, and he'd left the CIA to rid his life of deception. He took off the robe and climbed back into bed, feeling brutish and morose.

Until he flung out an arm and collided with cool, silky skin.

"What...?" he asked, propping up on an elbow.

"It's me," Athena said. "I know how you feel about me right now, but I thought you might want to talk about it."

He was still too angry to be conciliatory. "I thought we just did that. I'd like to sleep," he said, turning away. "Stay, if you like, just keep to your side."

"David, I'm sorry," she said sincerely, pulling on his arm to try to draw him onto his back. "Please. I don't know what else to say."

He pulled his arm away. "I understand that you're sorry," he said, his back to her. "You're sorry about a lot of things. Unfortunately, it's not enough this time. We just terrified your sister, and wasted a brilliant man's time because you didn't tell me the truth."

"I explained that!" she said loudly. "I kept meaning to tell you, but everything was so entangled, then I knew you'd be upset, so I was trying to pick the moment."

"And ruined everybody's night."

She bounced to a sitting position, turned on her bedside lamp and applied a stiff shove to his shoulder. "Sit up!" she ordered. "You're not going to just dismiss me like this."

He remained stubbornly where he lay. "It's almost midnight, Athena. Go to sleep."

She choked a bitter little laugh. "You know what, Hartford? You're more like your mother than you think."

If there was anything that could have turned him

from his determination to ignore her until morning, that was it. He sat up angrily and glared at her.

"What?" he demanded shortly.

"We compared notes on our mothers," she said, a pale vision in tumbled hair and white shoulders, the blanket clutched to the flimsy top of her nightgown. He hated that he noticed, but he couldn't help it. "You said they might have been separated at birth. Well, my mother always gave me what you're giving me now."

"What?" he asked. "Well-deserved hell?"

She pursed her mouth. "The cold shoulder. Sometimes I thought she liked me, then I'd do something foolish or wrong and she'd turn away as if I wasn't worth her trouble. Just like you're doing now. Is it because you got to make all those life-and-death decisions about other people in your work? You decide who's good and who's bad? Who's worth saving and who isn't?" She leaned right into his face. "Well, you know what I think?"

"I suppose this is one area," he said wryly, "in which I can count on you to tell the truth." Those life and death decisions had always been a problem for him, but the cause was just and he believed only cowards refused to make the tough decisions.

She put a hand to his heart. Every cell under her fingertips came alive in response. Sensory images of their lovemaking only hours ago roared through him, but he struggled to remain still.

"I think you can't forgive yourself, so you can't forgive me. Because I love you just as you are, despite all the things you've done that you want to forget—and those things you've told me still hurt. And that probably stops you from putting it all away, doesn't it? I love all of you, so I guess that keeps the past ever-present because it went to make you what you are.'' She dropped her hand and sighed defeatedly.

''I understand in a way,'' she went on, her expression softening. ''I've become what I am because of my mother—all tough and serious, concerned only with the struggle for justice. But sometimes we need more than fair play, don't we? We need softness, tolerance, understanding of who we are inside…under it all.'' She sighed again. ''Less than two weeks with you and I don't know who I am anymore. So, see? The deception wasn't entirely a trick.''

She climbed abruptly out of bed and stopped beside it to give him a sad smile. ''But maybe you're right. Love shouldn't be this confused. Good night, David.''

She left the room and closed the door behind her.

He stared at it, thinking in profanities as the sudden stillness of the room closed around him.

Damn her for thinking she could touch his heart and read what was in it.

Damn her for being right.

Chapter Fourteen

David gave Dotty a handful of cash. Alexis stood by the door, pulling on her black leather jacket. The boys had just returned from school and shot baskets while waiting for Dotty to take them to town to catch a matinee.

"How long do you want us to be gone?" Dotty asked worriedly. "And are you sure you're going to be all right alone with this Darby person?"

David knew her concern was genuine and tried not to smile. As far as she knew, his trips away from home over the years had been fishing trips with Trevyn. She didn't know he'd been trained to take on several men at once.

"I'll be fine."

"But if he's desperate for Brandon's money, he might become violent."

"I can handle that."

Athena appeared at his shoulder. "And *I'll* be here," she said, putting up two small fists as though she knew how to use them.

Alexis frowned. "Athena, please remember that you have a warrior's name but a rather slender woman's body. Please don't think bigger than you are." She glanced at David. "That's a problem with her, you know."

"Really," he said with a dry glance in Athena's direction. "I hadn't noticed."

Athena ignored him and walked Dotty and Lex to the door. "Maybe you should call before you come home," she said. "And can you bring home a couple of pizzas? That sounds really good to me."

"What if that Darby guy is still here?" Dotty asked.

"He won't be," Athena assured her. "Have a good time."

David stepped outside with her to wave the boys and the women off. He hadn't told the boys about Darby's visit because whatever happened, he was determined they weren't going back. And if he had to insure that outcome by pounding the message into Darby, he didn't want anyone there.

Athena, however, had been chirping around the house since receiving a fax about an hour ago. She'd been keeping her distance from him, but when he almost collided with her in the kitchen, she looked confident, even self-satisfied. When he'd asked her to share her plan again, she'd refused.

"All you have to do is follow my lead," she said.

"That's a lot to ask," he reminded, "of a man you've lied to on every front."

She'd sighed, her confidence slipping for a moment. "Well, this isn't about us, personally, is it? It's about legalities, and that's my turf."

He hadn't questioned her again, deciding to trust

her. Actually, it wasn't that difficult. He was having trouble sustaining his anger with her, anyway, even though he felt he still had a right to it. And she might want nothing to do with him now, but she cared about his brothers.

He doubted she'd understand his change of heart, though. She'd been right about him. It hurt to live with some of his past, and it made him curiously vulnerable to know she could love him anyway. Company agents spent every waking moment striving *not* to be vulnerable.

But he'd hurt her and she was keeping a polite but careful distance. When Darby arrived, though, Athena was standing right behind David. She was wearing her hair loose and he acknowledged that as a good ploy. She looked like an angel from whom there would be nothing to fear.

Darby was just the kind of man his mother would pick, David thought, studying the slick good looks, the pretentious ascot, the sophisticated air diminished by an underlying desperation.

David invited him inside, but he resisted, remaining in the doorway. "Are the boys ready?" he asked.

"The boys aren't here," David replied. "And they're not going anywhere with you. They're staying with me."

Darby looked him over, apparently considering his chances in a physical confrontation. In outward appearance they were evenly matched, but while Darby had spent his days in a computer chair, trading stocks, and his nights making bets, David had been climbing, crawling, fighting.

Darby glanced at his watch. "I'll be back with the police in an hour."

"Before you go to the police," Athena said in a pleasant, even tone of voice, "maybe we should talk."

Darby looked her up and down. "Who's she?"

"My lawyer," David replied.

"There's nothing to talk about," Darby said. "The children are my wife's and I'm filing for adoption. David has no legal custody."

"That's very true," Athena said.

David wanted to ask her what in the hell she was doing, but he'd promised to trust her and he intended to carry through.

Darby started to turn away toward his rental car, and Athena added, "But I think he could get custody if the court knew about the size of your gambling debts. Put that together with your stated intentions with Fitz, Holbein and Grosset to put you in charge of Brandon's trust fund and I'd say you look like a man who'd try to beat a child out of his money."

Darby gave her a scornful smile. "Good luck proving that."

Athena sighed defeatedly. "You're right. I couldn't prove that."

The only thing that prevented David from outright panic was the little glint in Athena's eyes. She was enjoying this, which led David to believe she was setting Darby up. He leaned against the molding and waited her out.

Darby made another turn to go to his car when Athena's voice stopped him again.

"But...Mr. Blakemore."

He turned back with strained patience. "Yes?"

She held up a sheaf of papers. "There are some things I *can* prove."

His expression changed slowly from smug satisfaction to mild concern. "What?"

She held the door open wider. "Why don't you come inside, so we can talk about it?"

He squared his shoulders and stood his ground. "You're bluffing, Miss Ames. I've done nothing that could be used against me in court."

"No, but it could be used against you with your wife, and if you don't have her, you don't have access to any of the perks you currently enjoy, regardless of Brandon's trust fund. Do you?"

Darby went white.

Athena made a sweeping invitation inside with the papers she held.

"You're bluffing," he accused, but he came into the living room.

Athena led him to the sofa, handed him several pages of the sheets she held, then stood near the coffee table and read from those in her hand.

"You might want to follow along with me, Darby," she said. "Because if you're going to have to defend yourself to Jordana, you'll want to make sure you have every base covered." She grinned wickedly as she shuffled through papers and glanced at him over the top. "Although, not being *covered*—" she emphasized the word to give it a different meaning "—seems to be a lot of your problem here, Darby, according to your 'headmistress,' Solana.''

Headmistress? David struggled to remain patient while wondering why Darby's complexion changed from white to ashen with overtones of crimson on his cheeks.

''Unlike many women in her line of work,'' Athena went on, sitting on the edge of the coffee table so she could place the pages in her lap, ''she doesn't seem to have a confidentiality code. Or maybe she's just waited too long for your payment.'' She followed along the page with the tip of a pen. ''Diana, a submissive, June 10. Two hours. Jeanette, June 13, dominant. Half an hour…''

David listened to her with growing respect for her tactics. A man's private life usually had aspects that could be used to an enemy's advantage. That's precisely what he'd have had Henry check out if he hadn't promised to let her handle it herself.

She smiled pleasantly at Darby. ''A lot harder to take what you dish out, isn't it? I guess that's just a fact of life. Jordana might even understand that. Let's see, where was I. Oh, here we are. Sarah… Mmm. I don't think I can even say that out loud. Three hours. Wow.''

She switched pages. ''Your bill for May and June at Solana's Grade School was in the high five figures. Does Jordana know that, Darby?'' Athena asked. ''Or does she really think you're losing *all* that money gambling?''

He looked enraged, then frightened, then fatalistically calm. "All right," he said finally. "The boys can stay."

"We want formal guardianship papers." She folded her arms atop the incriminating evidence, her voice quietly authoritative. "We want a phone call from Jordana no later than tomorrow telling us you've convinced her that leaving the boys with David is in everyone's best interest and that she's seeing an attorney about guardianship. After we get the paperwork, I'll destroy *this* paperwork, and your little pastime remains a secret."

"That's blackmail," he said.

She tapped her pen against her chin as though considering that. "Yeah," she said finally. "That's what I'd call it. So what do you say? Your continued freedom to remain Jordana's spoiled little pet while you indulge your bad habits behind her back, in exchange for the boys."

It was no contest. If he lost Jordana, he lost everything.

"All right." He got to his feet and started for the door. "How do I know you won't keep copies?" he demanded of David.

"Because I'm telling you we won't," he replied.

Darby shook his head and indicated Athena, who remained near the coffee table, squaring her papers on its top. "Where did you get this lawyer? From the Gambinos? Here!" He gave him back the copies of Solana's records, then brushed his hands on his coat as he fairly ran out the front door.

David turned to Athena, exultant, but she was still wearing her lawyer face. He had to tread carefully.

"I'm sorry," he said sincerely.

That seemed to puzzle her. She handed him the papers. "For what?"

He added them to the ones he held, then dropped the lot onto the coffee table. "For being so difficult about the triplet thing."

Her expression softened and she hitched a shoulder in a conciliatory gesture. "I should have taken more care to explain it to you before you found out the hard way."

He wanted to put his hands on her, but she continued to look uncertain, so he put them in his pockets instead. "No, I should have thought about the desperate means we're willing to take for those we love, and not focused on how it had affected me personally. Today, when you were willing to be hard-nosed and stretch to the edge for me, I got a different perspective." He smiled, unable to stop himself, when he looked down into her angel face. "You're pretty tough."

"I am," she admitted, knowing he had to be disappointed to find that out. He had a preference for the sweet woman she'd always wanted to be, not the dragon she'd patterned after her mother—the dragon who'd tricked him and lied to him and caused an enormous upheaval in his life. "So, that's the awful truth, Hartford. I'm more my mother's daughter than I've ever wanted to be. Now, if you'll excuse me…"

"Whoa." He caught her arm and held on. "That isn't her in you that makes you such a tough cookie when you're going after what you believe in. That's you—the sweet you who knows how to stand firm."

She thought about that, mulling over the words, startled by the possibility that they could be true.

"It's not her," he said again, as though knowing she had to hear it a second time. "It's you. Sweet and tough. All Athena—warrior woman and...angel all wrapped into one."

She felt paralyzed under the possibility.

It wasn't a legacy from her mother, it was just a part of herself? That was so simple.

"But you don't like her—the warrior woman, I mean. You like the woman who comes out when you kiss me."

"No," he said, clearly indignant that she thought so. He pulled her toward the stairs and sat down with her at about the same spot where they'd talked the night of the party.

"Listen to me," he said urgently, holding her hands. "There isn't a man alive who won't admit that he loves a woman who's warm and pliant in his arms, who comes alive when he touches her. But he'd be a fool if he didn't appreciate the one who can fight beside him as well.

"I was angry because I'd been tricked as part of your plan. It hurt my pride. But I like to think my intelligence runs deeper than pride. I love all of you, Athena. I love that you cared that much about your aunt that you and your sisters embarked upon a secret mission. That you wanted to get your sister back so much that you thought on your feet and came up with the best plan you could. I'm a street fighter myself."

Warmth filled every little corner of her being.

"About that..." he said, something shifting in his

eyes, bringing the darkness that invaded them when he talked about Company work. "You were right about me. It's a little scary to me to know what I am and to know that you love me anyway. That kind of generosity requires the same thing in return."

She squeezed his hands. "Everything you did, I know you did with pure intentions."

"Yeah," he said with a sigh. "Do you think intentions count?"

"You just told me that mine counted with you. So yours count with me. And I've seen examples of your generosity over and over again. With me, with the boys."

He brought her knuckles to his lips. "Then you can live with that? And help me fill this house with children and noisy parties?"

She had to close her eyes against the sudden brilliance of her life. She threw her arms around him. "Yes, I can. I can."

"I'll have the boys."

"I know. I got them for you, remember?"

He laughed and held her even tighter. "You were brilliant."

"It's a proven fact that someone crooked and seedy in one phase of his life is crooked and seedy in another. I took the chance, had Patrick check him out and...there it was in the old bank statements. A private account. That led him to the 'school's' current accounts receivable."

She nipped at his earlobe, then giggled as she hugged him. "I'm going to get to live here after all! Think of that! My sisters are going to be so thrilled."

She sobered just a little. "At least, I hope Gusty will be here eventually to *be* thrilled."

Athena swallowed back the tears and squared her shoulders.

"Meanwhile, we have to make a life for the boys," she said, leaning back to look into his face. "I love you, David. I'm sorry about all the tricks and the fibs, but I promise, from here on out—"

He didn't seem to have to hear the rest of the promise. "I love you, too," he interrupted, and kissed her soundly. Then he held her away from him and asked, "What about your practice?"

She hadn't really considered that, but the answer came to her quickly, simply. "I'll have to wrap up a few things, then I'll just move it to Dancer's Beach."

"That won't seem dull after D.C.?"

"No. This is home to me." She wrapped her arms around his neck again and held him tightly. "You're home to me."

They were still holding on to each other when Dotty, Lex and the boys came home with two large pizzas and a two-liter bottle of cola.

Brandon pulled Athena aside in the conservatory while Dotty and Alexis set the table. "Do we have to go back?" he asked anxiously.

When she expressed surprise that he'd suspected Darby was trying to reclaim them, he gave her a wry smile. "I checked the caller ID when Mom called that night. I knew Darby would try to get us back."

"He did." She felt obliged to be honest with him. "But he failed. Your mom's attorneys are sending us guardianship papers tomorrow."

He smiled and cocked an eyebrow. "Us?"

"Yeah. David and I are getting married. What do you think?"

"Married! Wow!" Brady, on his way into the room to report that dinner was ready, overheard Athena and raced back to the dining room to herald the news.

There were hugs and congratulations all around before they settled down to eat.

"That was pretty quick," Lex said, walking around the table, pouring soft drinks. "Has it been two weeks yet?"

David winked across the table at Athena, seated between the boys. "Actually, it's been since last February," he corrected. "I've thought about her all this time."

Alexis took her seat, looked into her sister's eyes, then David's and shook her head. "Trust you to find the one man in the world who's a romantic. The boys tell me you've sold a book."

"Not yet," David corrected. "I have a—" He stopped abruptly to catch Brady's hand as the boy reached over Alexis's plate to reach the red pepper flakes. "Ask someone to pass it to you," he admonished gently, then freed the boy's hand. He refocused on Alexis and continued. "I have a literary agent willing to take me on. So that's a step in the right direction."

"A big step," Alexis added. Teasingly she reached across Brady's plate to reclaim the pepper.

David said to Athena in a stage whisper, "She's going to be a good influence."

Athena rolled her eyes. ''When we got into trouble as children, it was usually her fault.''

''Oh, you two always wanted to go along,'' Alexis said. ''Because then it gave you someone to blame when things went wrong.'' She leaned conspiratorially toward David. ''I'm much maligned in this family, but if it wasn't for me, Gusty and Athena would have obeyed all the rules and never had any fun.''

''Don't listen to her,'' Athena advised David, ''or before you know it, you'll be up in a tree with no way down, or at the bottom of a cliff with no way up. She loves to put herself in impossible situations.''

Alexis frowned across the table at her sister. ''If you'll recall, I was forced into this one, I did not put myself into it.''

Athena raised both hands in surrender. ''True enough. And all my fault. There. You happy?''

Alexis smiled. ''Yeah. I liked that.'' She pulled a slice of vegetarian pizza from the platter in the middle of the table and put it on her plate. ''Are you two going to live here?''

Athena nodded.

''What about your practice in Washington?''

''We were just talking about that. I'll move it here as soon as David finishes the book and can come with me.''

''Are we coming?'' Brady asked.

Athena blinked. Of course. The boys. No more taking off on a moment's notice. ''Ah, can they?'' she asked David.

He looked doubtful. ''They should probably stay in school. Dotty's here.''

Brady groaned. "We never get a break about school!"

David laughed. "We'll do something special when we get back."

"But you can't go," Brandon put in, "until we find the other sister, can you?"

Athena was unsure how to respond to that.

Alexis did it for her. "Of course they can. I'll be here to hold down the fort and you guys can help me." She smiled from Brandon to Brady. "The sooner Athena gets her office moved, the sooner your lives will be organized. What else can we do about Gusty?"

"I've got a good friend from my CIA days working on it," David said. Alexis nodded. Athena had explained what had been responsible for the curious absences in their biographical information. "And Athena and I have been up and down the coast. I think all we can do now is wait for some sign of her."

Alexis looked dissatisfied with that answer.

"I know," Athena said sympathetically. "I hate it, too. But there's always the hope she'll remember something and come here or go home or get in touch with one of us."

Alexis made a face. "I've never been very good at sitting and waiting, but we don't have many alternatives, do we? The boys and I can do some fun stuff while you're gone."

"Like what?" Brady wanted to know.

"Like making scarecrows for the front porch, going to Dancer's Beach for sundaes, hiking the nature trail behind the park."

Both boys looked interested.

Alexis nodded at David. "That's settled. After you send away the rest of your manuscript, you're free to take off and I'll help Dotty with the boys."

"HOW DID SUCH A WONDERFUL THING happen?" Athena asked David later when everyone else had gone to bed and they sat on the sofa in front of the fire. "How did love find us in the middle of such a frightening and worrisome situation as the disappearance of my sister?"

He sat with his legs stretched out and his feet propped on the coffee table, Athena reclining in his lap.

"I don't think love finds you," he replied, stroking her hair. "I think we found it. Both of us needed something we found in each other. And meeting each other's needs is…love."

She liked that notion. "What did you find in me?"

"Guts," he replied. "Cleverness, laughter, a willingness to love me."

She liked that, too. "Do you know what I found in you?"

He tugged playfully on her hair. "Careful now."

She smiled up at him. "Oh, you'll like this. I found everything I dreamed about as a girl when Gusty and Lex and I were at home with our mother and hating our lives and living for the day we could make our own families. Strength, shelter, kindness, affection."

He squeezed her closer. "You'll want a reprieve from affection before I'm done with you."

"Never." She sat up to wrap her arms around his

neck. "One day I'm going to introduce you to Gusty," she said firmly.

"Yes, you will," he agreed. "And she and Alexis can keep a room here and come whenever they want. So they'll always be part of our family." He looked gently into her eyes. "Can you think about marrying me before we find her?"

She expected the very idea to fill her with regret that she would take such an important step without Gusty. But the thought of being David's wife gave her such a sense of wholeness that she felt happy rather than sad.

"I can. And I think we should do it right here in the living room, before we go east."

David kissed her soundly. "That was the right answer," he said, getting to his feet, then lifting her into his arms. "And I have only one thing to say in response."

He carried her silently upstairs, his answer requiring no words.

Epilogue

Alexis Ames wandered into the dark kitchen, flipped on the light and blinked against the sudden brightness. The clock above the stove said 2:17 a.m.

Great. Insomnia had made the transatlantic trip with her. Although she'd slept soundly the night before, apparently she was experiencing a delayed reaction to jet lag.

Thinking that some of the peach tea Dotty had made her the night before might help, she filled the kettle and put it on to boil.

She rummaged in the cookie jar for an oatmeal raisin to go with her tea.

Reaching into an overhead cupboard for a cup, she noticed that the kitchen light lit the hallway, and knew that Dotty slept in a room at the end of it.

She quickly put the tea bag into the cup, then flipped the light off and settled in a kitchen chair with her cookie, waiting for the water to boil.

Her mind went immediately to Gusty, but she pushed the thought away, unable to bear another moment of worry. She prayed, she sent love her sister's way every moment of every day. But she had to think about something else or she would go mad.

She planned a trip to town to sketch the old hotel, the library building in the park, the downtown with its old buildings and streetlights with hanging flower bas—

A noise at the back door brought her instantly out of her thoughts. A cat? she wondered. A raccoon?

It came again, quietly but deliberately—like a key in a lock, but not quite.

A burglar! It wouldn't be the first time Cliffside had attracted one. Sadie had once wandered downstairs in her sleeping mask and frightened two teenage intruders into surrendering without a struggle.

Alexis crept to the stove and felt for the frying pan Dotty always left on the right rear burner.

From across the room came the efficient click of an opened lock. Alexis hid behind the refrigerator, her heart in her throat.

As she did so, her brain chided her. "Why don't you just shout for David? Why don't you turn on the light? Why don't you just scream?" Any of those plans of action would certainly have discouraged a burglar.

Yeah, well, that was her problem. She acted before she thought. That quality had plagued her her entire life. Hopefully, she would live through this so that it could do so again.

The door opened with a slow creak, then was closed quietly.

Footsteps moved stealthily across the kitchen, toward the refrigerator.

Punk, Alexis thought. Crime reports were always filled with stories of thieves who helped themselves to food while they burgled.

Slowly, her heartbeat about to strangle her, she moved around the refrigerator door and lifted the frying pan in both hands.

She caught a glimpse of the back of a dark head, square shoulders in a gray sweatshirt, and a tight backside in faded jeans as she swung the pan.

An instant before it connected, the man spun around, caught her wrist, hooked her foot with his and dropped her to the floor.

She screamed, the pan went flying and crashed into something that made a terrible racket. She lay on the cold hardwood floor, the man kneeling astride her waist, one of his hands covering her mouth.

She bucked and flailed, unable to believe that she could suffer this kind of treatment twice in two days.

Her wrists were pinned in one of his when the overhead light went on, blinding her.

"What in the...?" she heard David's voice demand.

"This woman attacked me," said the man astride her. "I just walked into the kitchen and she—" He stopped abruptly, muttered an oath, then exclaimed, "Augusta!"

Alexis squinted up at him, the light too bright to allow her to see.

"Where's the baby?" he asked, his voice filled with a sort of surprised wonder.

David groaned. "Here we go again. Trev, this is Alexis."

"Who?"

"Alexis. Augusta's sister. And this is Athena."

Alexis heard a startled gasp, then the man said in a panicked voice, "Jeez! Am I losing it?"

"Yes," David replied, "but not about this. They're triplets. Let her up, Trev."

"Oh." The man rose off her and two strong hands pulled her deftly to her feet.

She blinked to clear light spots from her eyes and looked into a handsome, angular face with inky dark eyes and a mouth with a decidedly devilish twist to it.

He dusted off the shoulder of her pink chenille robe. "I'm sorry," he said. "But you were going to bean me with a frying pan."

"Because you broke into the house!" she replied a little hotly, embarrassed by the amused expressions of David, Athena and Dotty. Mercifully, the boys hadn't awakened.

"I didn't *break* in," he tried to explain. "I misplaced my key and I…"

"So you picked the lock?" she demanded. "Who are you that you know how to do that?"

"He's my friend, Trevyn McGinty, Lex," David said. "He lives in the guest house and often lets himself in to borrow my groceries when he comes back from a long shoot."

"You can't just knock?" Alexis asked.

"It's late," he said defensively. "I didn't want to wake anyone."

David indicated the smashed crockery in the drying rack. "Well, that didn't work. I've been trying to reach you for days. You finished with the calendar commission?''

''Yeah.'' Trevyn grew suddenly grim. ''When I crossed into Washington, I saw Augusta's photo on the news and hurried home.''

Athena, Alexis and David looked at each other. Alexis knew they had their answer.

''I'm the father of her baby,'' Trevyn said.

* * * * *

Don't miss

FATHER FORMULA,
by Muriel Jensen,

Book Two of the
WHO'S THE DADDY? *series.*

Coming next month
from Harlequin American Romance.

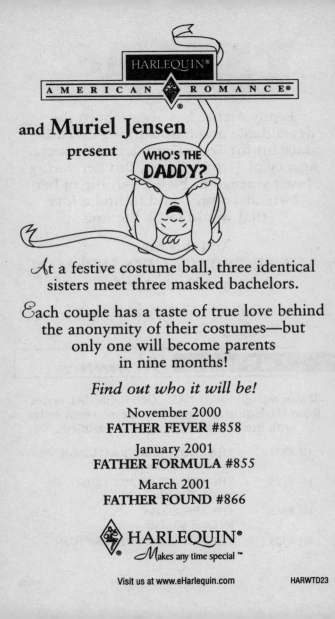

TEXAS CONFIDENTIAL

Penny Archer has always been the
dependable and hardworking executive
assistant for Texas Confidential, a secret
agency of Texas lawmen. But her daring
heart yearned to be the heroine of her
own adventure—and to find a love
that would last a lifetime.

And this time...
THE SECRETARY GETS HER MAN
by Mindy Neff

Coming in January 2001 from

◆ HARLEQUIN®

AMERICAN *Romance*

If you missed the TEXAS CONFIDENTIAL series
from Harlequin Intrigue, you can place an order
with our Customer Service Department.

Tyler Brides

It happened one weekend...

Quinn and Molly Spencer are delighted to accept three bookings for their newly opened B&B, Breakfast Inn Bed, located in America's favorite hometown, Tyler, Wisconsin.

But Gina Santori is anything but thrilled to discover her best friend has tricked her into sharing a room with the man who broke her heart eight years ago....

And Delia Mayhew can hardly believe that she's gotten herself locked in the Breakfast Inn Bed basement with the sexiest man in America.

Then there's Rebecca Salter. She's turned up at the Inn in her wedding gown. Minus her groom.

Come home to Tyler for three delightful novellas by three of your favorite authors: Kristine Rolofson, Heather MacAllister and Jacqueline Diamond.

HARLEQUIN®
Makes any time special ™

Arriving this December from

TWIN EXPECTATIONS
by
Kara Lennox

Identical twins Liz and Bridget Van Zandt always
dreamed of marrying and starting families at the
same time. But with their biological clocks ticking
loudly and no suitable husbands in sight, the
sisters decided it was time to take action.

Their new agenda: Have babies without
the benefit of grooms. They never expected
they'd meet two eligible bachelors whose
destinies were about to crash headlong
into their carefully laid plans....

Don't miss the fun and excitement in this special
two-stories-in-one volume from **Kara Lennox**
and **Harlequin AMERICAN *Romance*!**

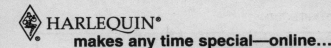

HARLEQUIN®
makes any time special—online...

eHARLEQUIN.com

shop eHarlequin

- ♥ Find all the new Harlequin releases at everyday great discounts.
- ♥ Try before you buy! Read an excerpt from the latest Harlequin novels.
- ♥ Write an online review and share your thoughts with others.

reading room

- ♥ Read our Internet exclusive daily and weekly online serials, or vote in our interactive novel.
- ♥ Talk to other readers about your favorite novels in our Reading Groups.
- ♥ Take our Choose-a-Book quiz to find the series that matches you!

authors' alcove

- ♥ Find out interesting tidbits and details about your favorite authors' lives, interests and writing habits.
- ♥ Ever dreamed of being an author? Enter our Writing Round Robin. The Winning Chapter will be published online! Or review our guidelines for submitting your novel.

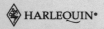

AMERICAN *Romance*

This small Wisconsin town
has some big secrets...and the
newest scandal is about to hit!

RETURN
TO
TYLER

SECRET BABY SPENCER
by Jule McBride
11/00 AR #849

PATCHWORK FAMILY
by Judy Christenberry
12/00 AR #853

**PRESCRIPTION FOR
SEDUCTION**
by Darlene Scalera
2/01 AR #861

BRIDE OF DREAMS
by Linda Randall Wisdom
3/01 AR #865

And in January 2001, be sure to look for this special
3-in-1 collection from Harlequin Books!

TYLER BRIDES
by Kristine Rolofson
Heather MacAllister
Jacqueline Diamond

*Warm as a cherished family quilt and bright
as a rainbow, these stories weave together
the fabric of a community.*

Available at your favorite retail outlet.

HARLEQUIN®
Makes any time special ™

Visit us at www.eHarlequin.com

HARRTT